AMERICAN POETS PROJECT

AMERICAN POETS PROJECT

IS PUBLISHED WITH A GIFT IN MEMORY OF

James Merrill

AND SUPPORT FROM ITS FOUNDING PATRONS

Sidney J. Weinberg, Jr. Foundation

The Berkley Foundation

Richard B. Fisher and Jeanne Donovan Fisher

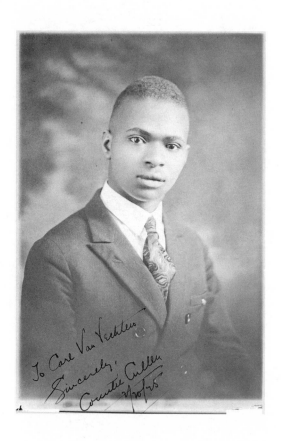

To Carl Van Vechten
Sincerely,
Countee Cullen
1925

Countee Cullen

COLLECTED POEMS —

EDITED BY
MAJOR JACKSON

AMERICAN POETS PROJECT

THE LIBRARY OF AMERICA

Introduction, volume compilation, and biographical note copyright © 2013 by
Literary Classics of the United States, Inc. All rights reserved. Printed in the
United States of America. No part of this book may be reproduced in any manner
whatsoever without permission.

Poems copyright © 2013 by Amistad Research Center, Tulane University.
For further information see the Note on the Texts and Illustrations.

The paper used in this publication meets the minimum requirements of the
American National Standard for Information Sciences—Permanence of Paper for
Printed Library Materials, ANSI Z39.48—1984.

Design by Chip Kidd and Mark Melnick.
Library of Congress Control Number: 2010924276
ISBN 978-1-59853-083-4
American Poets Project–32

10 9 8 7 6 5 4 3 2 1

CONTENTS

INTRODUCTION

From Phyllis Wheatley right up to our own ostensibly "postracial" moment, African American poets have had to bear a seemingly inescapable burden. Above and beyond the usual demands and privileges of the poetic vocation—for those fortunate enough to have been allowed to write poetry at all, and to have succeeded in the struggle—their work has had to do a kind of double duty. For black poets, merely wrestling with words and the mysteries of existence hasn't been considered enough, unless their efforts have also addressed race itself—unless they have come to terms in one way or another, as poets, with their "blackness."

This burden is evident in the apparent paradox of what is probably Countee Cullen's most famous couplet, from his first volume, *Color*:

> Yet do I marvel at this curious thing:
> To make a poet black, and bid him sing!

Even as Cullen's speaker marvels at the fact of his calling he also hesitates, noting that "poet" and "black" seem a "curious" or even potentially antithetical combination. These lines question and affirm simultaneously: a black poet discovers, quizzically but not unhappily, that he is both, and in doing so silences any doubt that the two terms belong together. And yet the speaker's momentary befuddlement at the idea that black people might write poetry also suggests a consciousness not quite at ease in its own skin. He marvels at himself, just as Phyllis Wheatley's interlocutors marveled at her some hundred and fifty years earlier, refusing to believe she had actually written her poems until she was able to answer their questions about them in person. And so, along with love, death, beauty, the absurdity of life, and whatever else, race becomes an obligatory theme for Cullen and for black American poets more generally. And their handling of "race," among some critics and readers, becomes a matter of major or even peremptory concern.

Cullen's career is a case in point rather than an exception to this rule. In his lifetime and after, his writings have been by turns excessively praised or prejudicially discounted, not so much for their particular literary merits or failings, but for the ways in which they address broader debates about race in American culture. Some, like W.E.B. Du Bois, sought to boost Cullen less for his art alone than for what his art would prove about African American character. Others, like Langston Hughes and many after him, suspected Cullen of aspiring to a kind of whiteness in his poetic practice—even as his poems articulate a unique vision of the joys and trials of being black, male, and some would vigorously add "gay" in early twentieth-century America.

In a publishing career that spanned over twenty years, Cullen produced a body of work that included not only five volumes of poetry—*Color* (1925), *Copper Sun* (1927), *The Black Christ, and Other Poems* (1929), *The Medea, and Some Poems* (1935), and the collected *On These I Stand*

(1947)—but also a novel, *One Way to Heaven* (1934); two children's books, *The Lost Zoo* and *My Nine Lives and How I Lost Them*; and the musical play *St. Louis Woman* (1946), his collaboration with poet and novelist Arna Bontemps. His translation of Euripides's *Medea* is considered the first major translation of a classical work by a black American writer. The present volume also includes a number of poems Cullen left uncollected or unpublished, from hard-to-find little magazines and private journals and letters.

In the pages that follow, I hope to show some of the ways in which debates about the role of the black artist are impressed on the very texture and tone of Cullen's verse, and how he bore the pressures of exemplarity conferred on him in the wake of his early successes. It may be difficult to appreciate Cullen fully without some understanding of these concerns. They inform his language as surely as any metrical pattern or rhyme scheme. And yet I do not believe that Cullen's poems should be reduced to mere ciphers—in an argument, say, about the history of African American self-representation in a racist nation. After all such arguments are done and forgotten, Cullen's poems will still be able to give great pleasure on their own terms. Fortified by his deep awareness of the Bible and English literature, not to mention the classical and French writers he loved to translate, and stimulated by the technical challenges of his chosen medium, Cullen left a body of poetry that offers us, if nothing else, a curious, marvelous, and singular self-portrait.

* * *

Cullen's early years are as obscure, in their own way, as Phyllis Wheatley's African origins. He kept the true circumstances of his birth a secret from all but a few close friends and deliberately rewrote his past. Officially, he was Countee Cullen, or sometimes rather stylishly *Countée*.

(He dropped the accent for his published books of poetry, but used it in personal correspondence; it appears on his tombstone.) Born in New York (he often claimed), Countee Cullen came to be known as the son of one of Harlem's most influential men, the Reverend Frederick Asbury Cullen, pastor of the famed Salem Methodist Episcopal Church, and his wife Carolyn. He was raised in the parsonage of the church—a fine structure, still standing on the corner of Seventh Avenue and 129th Street, at the epicenter of many Harlem happenings. Along with the physical and emotional stability of a loving home, the Cullens provided a solid, conservative Christian upbringing. They were on the upper end of Harlem's burgeoning middle class.

In fact, Cullen was probably born Countee Lucas, in Louisville, Kentucky, or thereabouts, on May 30, 1903. In 1940, according to his widow Ida Mae Roberson, he attended and paid for the Louisville funeral of his mother, Elizabeth Thomas Lucas. But the two seem to have had little contact. Extreme poverty or some local scandal may have forced her to give him up; we can only speculate. He was raised by a grandmother or family friend, Amanda Porter, in the New York area. In 1918, a year after she died, he was unofficially adopted by the Cullens—perhaps because he had shown himself to be a particularly bright student at an early age. As he grew older, Countee began to question some of the more unreconstructed values and manners of his foster parents, but he remained a dutiful son until the end. Well into adulthood, he accompanied the Rev. Cullen on nearly annual summer trips, to Europe or the Holy Land, and after Carolyn Cullen died, he took his father in. He was evidently grateful for all they had given him. Yet they also provided him, like many parents, with an ample dose of psychic tension—a tension that would come into play in his writing.

Describing himself in a biographical note to *Caroling Dusk: An Anthology of Verse by Black Poets*—a groundbreaking Harlem Renaissance anthology he edited in 1927—Cullen offered a wry, telling account of his conflicted state: "Countée Cullen's chief problem has been that of reconciling a Christian upbringing with a pagan inclination." *Pagan* is a densely loaded term here. On the most polite level, it indicates Cullen's tendency, in his poetry, toward a kind of Keatsian sensualism. Instead of the moral strictures or exhortations one might find in a properly "Christian" poet—and indeed Cullen's father perennially urged him to write more poems in an explicitly devotional, religious mode—Cullen is more often interested in gorgeous imagery, or in the pleasures of the sounds of words for their own sake. (Critics have identified Keats as one of Cullen's primary influences, and indeed Cullen's tone often strikes one as exceptionally Keatsian. His lyrics often address the principal themes one associates with Keats: beauty, love, mortality. But what might be called Cullen's Keatsianism is intertwined and melded with other thematic concerns— particularly race, and wrestling with issues of doubt and faith. Cullen's "Christian upbringing" shows through, throughout his writings.)

Cullen's use of *pagan* may also raise the possibility that he sensed or wondered, as an African American poet, about some essential persistence of what Phyllis Wheatley called "my *Pagan* land"—an African past, or a specifically racial heritage, that would perhaps cut against the proprieties of his American, Christian life. Cullen sometimes rhapsodized over African scenes, offering exotic visions of magical, pantheistic worship in dark humid jungles. In "Heritage," he interrogates and examines the claims such visions ought to have on him. At one point he notes his distance from the "pagan" past:

> Here no bodies sleek and wet,
> Dripping mingled rain and sweat,
> Tread the savage measures of
> Jungle boys and girls in love.

Writing from the parsonage of Salem Methodist Episcopal, in his strictly iambic and certainly never "savage" measures, Cullen is by turns fascinated by, distressed over, and even occasionally embarrassing in his enthusiasm for what he imagines of "pre-Christian" Africa.

Pagan may also hint, at a more deeply coded level, of some self-awareness of homosexual identity. Gay writers and theorists beginning around the turn of the nineteenth century often turned to ancient Greece as a way to find their roots and imagine a less encumbered future, just as many black writers turned to Africa. Cullen avidly followed both of these intellectual developments, reading and making contacts with proponents of both. In 1922, writing to Alain Locke—a leading Howard University intellectual and fellow traveler in both camps—he described his response to the gay utopian Edward Carpenter's Greek-themed *Ioläus* (1917):

> I read it through at one sitting, and steeped myself in its charming and comprehending atmosphere. It opened up for me soul windows which had been closed; it threw a noble and evident light on what I had begun to believe, because of what the world believes, ignoble and unnatural. I loved myself in it.

Throughout his poetry, and perhaps also in his private life, Cullen tentatively explored the "pagan" side of his divided identity, and questioned some of the orthodoxies within which he was raised. But from the beginning Cullen was a poet with a public reputation—a kind of prodigy, whose works were noticed and held up for praise. If he attempted to reconcile the "Christian" and "pagan" elements of his personality, it was in poems intended for the widest possible public consumption, not a coterie audience. The burdens of exemplarity began early. In high school—the almost exclusively white DeWitt Clinton High School, where he served as the editor of the school newspaper and assistant editor to the school's literary magazine *The Magpie*—he began to be recognized for his literary talents. He won his first of many contests, a citywide competition sponsored by the Federation of Women's Clubs, with his poem "I Have a Rendezvous with Life" (1920)—a poetic reply to Alan Seeger's then-popular poem of World War I, "I Have a Rendezvous with Death" (1916). It begins:

> I have a rendezvous with life,
> In days I hope will come,
> Ere youth has sped and strength of mind;
> Ere voices sweet grow dumb;
> I have a rendezvous with life,
> When spring's first heralds hum.

Though not perhaps a poem for the ages—only five years later, when he published his first book, *Color*, Cullen omitted this early work—"I Have a Rendezvous" marked an auspicious beginning. In its moment, the poem was a minor hit, published in New York's (white) daily newspapers, and soon reprinted in magazines and anthologies. One writer, Gaius Glenn Atkins, borrowed Cullen's phrase for the title of his own book, *A Rendezvous with Life* (1922). Indeed, Cullen scholar Gerald Early has suggested that Cullen's precocious debut—rather than, say, the publication of Jean Toomer's *Cane* in 1923—ought to mark the beginning of what we now know as the Harlem Renaissance. This may seem a heavy weight of expectation to rest on a poem that is nothing if not light and cheerful, but it accurately reflects the eagerness with which young black writers were being looked to for signs of uplift and revitalization.

It was the appearance of his poem "The Shroud of Color" in H. L. Mencken's *American Mercury* in November 1924 that first propelled Cullen onto the national literary scene and made him one of the most talked-about black writers in the country. He "became famous, like Byron, overnight," Mencken later recalled. The 199-line poem, mainly in iambic rhyming couplets, begins with a speaker in crisis. "[B]eing dark," he "cannot bear" to go on living, and very melodramatically throws himself, groaning, onto the earth, asking God to let him die. God instead reveals a vast cosmic vision—a vision which enables him to understand his suffering as a source of strength, and to find solidarity in the suffering of his people:

> And somehow it was borne upon my brain
> How being dark, and living through the pain
> Of it, is courage more than angels have. I knew
> What storms and tumults lashed the tree that grew
> This body that I was, this cringing I
> That feared to contemplate a changing sky,
> This I that grovelled, whining, "Let me die,"
> While others struggled in Life's abattoir.
> The cries of all dark people near or far
> Were billowed over me, a mighty surge
> Of suffering in which my puny grief must merge
> And lose itself; I had no further claim to urge
> For death; in shame I raised my dust-grimed head,

And though my lips moved not, God knew I said,
"Lord, not for what I saw in flesh or bone
Of fairer men; not raised on faith alone;
Lord, I will live persuaded by mine own.
I cannot play the recreant to these;
My spirit has come home, that sailed the doubtful seas."

The poem struck many readers as a tour de force, not only for its perspective on race relations in America but for the virtuosity with which it cast the struggle and plight of "all dark people," both aesthetically and thematically, in high Miltonic terms. It is a kind of blues poem, written in the key of *Paradise Lost*. It not only discovers and asserts a sense of racial solidarity, but does so in a grand and "epic" manner, against the presumptions of a white audience. Cullen's diction alone seems a repudiation of racist typecasting, and goes out of its way to insist on his seriousness.

Cullen's debut volume, *Color*, was published by Harper & Row in 1925, the year he graduated from New York University. It was perhaps the most auspicious and long-awaited first book in African American literature, and it sold more than two thousand copies in its first two years in print. It confirmed what many, seeing his poems in magazines, had already begun to suspect: Cullen was one of the major writers of his generation, another star in the expanding literary universe that came to be known as the Harlem Renaissance, along with figures like Langston Hughes, Zora Neale Hurston, Claude McKay, and Jean Toomer. As a result of his resolve to master the high literary tradition of poetry, Cullen emerged in the mid-1920s critically acclaimed by both black and white readers.

It is little wonder, given Cullen's then-prominence, that two of the most enduring critical statements from the Harlem Renaissance on the function of African American creative expression should take Cullen as their starting point: Du Bois's "Criteria of Negro Art" and Langston Hughes's "The Negro Artist and the Racial Mountain." Cullen was celebrated as the golden exemplar of a campaign by black political and cultural leaders who sought to engineer a new image of black people in America. Yet he was also targeted as an aesthete, and his expressed desire to be read as "a poet and not a Negro poet" was increasingly condemned as representative of black aristocratic self-hatred, and worse, a veiled longing "to be white." To his critics, it did not matter or help that Cullen wrote some of the most formally adept American verse of the decade. Instead, his poems engaged traditional (read "white") literary modes with altogether too much enthusiasm, and seemed sponsored in sound and sense by a bygone era. His penchant for penning pitch-perfect sonnets and jaunty ballad stanzas (so accomplished that he would later pick up the nickname "the Black Keats") was both blessing and curse in an age that had stopped its metronome and begun to favor the various iconoclasms of modernism over mastery of tradition, and the raw potential of black vernacular forms over seemingly exhausted Anglo-American gentilities.

Du Bois—the leading black intellectual of the early twentieth century and recognized leader of what he called "the Talented Tenth"—valued Cullen's literary achievements and example immensely, for they signaled the arrival of a black man who could play the English language like a song and engage with literary tradition as well as any white poet. In an address delivered in June 1926 at the Chicago Conference of the NAACP, Du Bois recounted the story of a University of Chicago professor who recited an excerpt of a poem and then asked his literature students to identify the author. Du Bois reports: "They guessed a goodly company from Shelley and Robert Browning to Tennyson and Masefield. The author was Countée Cullen." One can almost hear Du Bois's near swoon, his self-satisfied pride at Cullen being mistaken for some of the most celebrated white poets in English literature. These conference remarks would be published later that year as "Criteria of Negro Art" in the NAACP's official magazine *The Crisis*, of which Du Bois served as editor; they would come to be a touchstone in debates over the role and purpose of the arts in the African American struggle for civil rights and social equality. "I do not care a damn for any art that is not used for propaganda," Du Bois proclaimed, and he celebrated black art for its unique role in promoting the truth of human equality and unmasking the lie of white supremacy. That Cullen's poetry could so easily be confused with that of Shelley or Browning or Tennyson confirmed for Du Bois some of his most closely held beliefs. He doggedly believed African Americans were equal to their white countrymen in all aspects of life, and Cullen was consummate proof.

James Weldon Johnson—poet, diplomat, and central member of the Talented Tenth—proposes a similar role for the black poet in the preface to his groundbreaking anthology, *The Book of American Negro Poetry* (1922). Like Du Bois, Johnson articulates the high yield black leaders expected of their artists and writers:

> No people that has produced great literature and art has ever been looked upon by the world as distinctly inferior. The status of the Negro in the United States is more a question of national mental attitude toward the race than of actual conditions. And nothing will do more to change that mental

attitude and raise his status than a demonstration of intellectual parity by the Negro through the production of literature and art.

In short, according to these representatives of the Talented Tenth, Cullen and other Harlem Renaissance poets were to be held responsible not only for counting syllables and contemplating the themes they wished to contemplate, but for the ways in which their efforts would lift up the race, and help to change the country's attitudes about African Americans.

To understand Du Bois's and Johnson's zeal for such a programmatic view of black art and their excitement over what they viewed as the import of Cullen's poetic achievement—Johnson, too, promoted Cullen and his career—one must keep in mind some of the battles they were fighting, from Harlem, as Cullen was coming of age in the late 1910s and early 1920s. For generations, a campaign of fear and racial violence had been waged against African Americans—an ugly scar on the American psyche which saw thousands of black people lynched, shot, or burned, in a horrific reign of brutality. Resistance to this campaign was necessarily ongoing. In the wake of D. W. Griffith's *Birth of a Nation* in 1915, the KKK had re-emerged. In 1922, the Dyer anti-lynching bill, which would have made lynching a federal crime, passed the House of Representatives but was blocked by white Southerners in the Senate. Against the backdrop of these and many similar incidents, Du Bois and other concerned African Americans (including Cullen's foster father, who organized anti-lynching protests and traveled to Washington to petition President Wilson in the wake of a race riot) found determination and purpose in substantiating black people's humanity above the status of hunted animals to be dragged up a tree and left to swing long after the mob had dissipated. "Negro Art," in such circumstances, could not exist for its own sake. It became a weapon, and a shield, against organized oppression. (Cullen himself, in 1922, published a searing anti-lynching poem, "Christ Recrucified," in a Harlem little magazine. He chose not to include it in *Color* or any of his later books, but it is reprinted here on page 238.)

One must realize, too, the particular appeal that highly decorous and elevated language would have had for Du Bois and other black critics. The black vernacular traditions that were just beginning to fascinate younger writers in the 1920s, like Zora Neale Hurston and Langston Hughes, could easily have seemed tainted, corrupt, or degrading, because they had been so thoroughly co-opted in racist white popular entertainments. For generations, the image of the Jim Crow "minstrel" and its many subsequent variations and iterations had presented black folk as simple-minded, uncouth, happy-go-lucky, and quick to a tune. Such dehumanizing stereotypes had found their way into the culture they parodied and mocked. Even a poet as proficient and accomplished as Paul Laurence Dunbar had had to "wear the mask" that others expected of him, writing in folksy dialect to appeal to white readers. Propriety and formality were antidotes to years of misrepresentations which reveled in the contrary. As Alain Locke put it in 1925, in his essay "Enter the New Negro":

> The day of "aunties," "uncles" and "mammies" is equally gone. Uncle Tom and Sambo have passed on, and even the "Colonel" and "George" play barnstorm roles from which they escape when the public spotlight is off. The popular melodrama has about played itself out, and it is time to scrap the fictions.

Cullen helped put such fictions on the scrap heap. In a rave review of *Color* in *The Crisis*, Du Bois singles out Cullen's ability to move beyond such simple typecasting:

> In a time when it is the vogue to make much of the Negro's aptitude for clownishness or to depict him objectively as a serio-comic figure, it is a fine and praiseworthy act for Mr. Cullen to show through the interpretation of his own subjectivity the inner workings of the Negro soul and mind.

Always impeccably tailored, not only was Cullen an anti-type of the minstrel show buffoon in his personal demeanor; his literary style seemed freshly free of the melodramatic, role-playing masks that Dunbar, Locke, and Du Bois lamented. It was a style transparent to his "inner workings," true to his dignity, rather than a performance put on for others. In 1925, he graduated Phi Beta Kappa from NYU, then went on to earn a master's degree in English and French from Harvard University, which made him, as one critic has noted, the most considerably educated black poet in America. He was also one of the most lauded, winning a succession of national prizes including the Witter Bynner Poetry contest, the John Reed Memorial Prize from *Poetry* magazine, and the Amy Spingarn Award of *The Crisis* magazine, among others. He did this not only without affecting a "serio-comic" or other sham-vernacular voice, but indeed in verse that owed more, it can be argued, to English literary tradition than to any American vernacular whatsoever, black or white. As other Harlem Renaissance writers like Langston Hughes and Jean Toomer began to participate in the avant-garde literary movements now known as modernism, Cullen pursued traditional forms with particular enthusiasm, not only writing ballads and sonnets and Spenserian stanzas, but also becoming, according to Robert Hillyer, the first American to publish a poem ("To Lovers of Earth: Fair Warning") in the antique, Chaucerian "rime royal." He was a formalist's formalist.

Members of the Talented Tenth were committed to celebrating Cullen's accomplishments, and he became a kind of standard-bearer for the race. Probably no one rejoiced more in Cullen's successes than Du Bois; indeed, his regard for the young poet was so high that he encouraged him to take his daughter's hand in marriage. The wedding of Countee Cullen and Nina Yolande Du Bois, on April 9, 1928, is now legendary for its extravagance. Langston Hughes later remembered it, in *The Big Sea* (1940), as "the social-literary event of the season, and very society." Officiated by the groom's father at Salem Methodist Episcopal Church—the large hall filled to capacity, and hundreds of uninvited onlookers crowding the streets outside—it represented a symbolic passing of the torch from the old guard of black political leaders to the new crop of young black artists and writers in attendance, the force and energy behind much of the fervor and excitement of the Harlem Renaissance. With his multiple accomplishments, Cullen offered exactly the kind of image that the Talented Tenth wished to project, and indeed immediately following the wedding, he took time out to address a race rally, postponing his honeymoon. He was at the height, perhaps, of his public career.

In the end, the wedding was more show than substance. Yolande, it is rumored, would have preferred to marry Jimmie Lunceford—a jazz musician with whom she is reported to have been infatuated. Cullen had already begun to understand himself as attracted to other men. They soon divorced, in 1930. Langston Hughes—who chafed, at the wedding, in his rented tux—was beginning to stake out his own distinct claims to the title of black laureate, and to seek new directions for African American poetry. Hughes and Cullen had been friends early in their roughly contemporary poetic careers, and they remained on relatively good terms throughout their lives, though they were competitors; they had many common friends and influences, including Howard professor Alain Locke. But in his landmark essay "The Negro Artist and the Racial Mountain," which appeared in *The Nation* in the same month as Du Bois's Chicago conference address, Hughes spurned Cullen's, and indeed black elites', "desire to run away spiritually from [their] race." He noted with palpable antipathy "this urge within the race toward whiteness, the desire to pour racial individuality into the mold of American standardization, and to be as little Negro and as much American as possible." And though he refrained from directly naming Cullen—instead speaking of "one of the most promising of the young Negro poets" who wished to be identified as a "poet—not a Negro poet"—the example of Cullen and his career was his point of departure. (Cullen had proclaimed defiantly in a 1924 interview in the *Brooklyn Daily Eagle*: "if I am going to be a poet at all, I am going to be POET and not NEGRO POET." As poet Gregory Pardlo has recently observed, Hughes leaves Cullen unmentioned partly because "it is polite to do so," but also because he finds Cullen's admission "so damaging.")

In Hughes's view, Cullen's insistence on distinguishing himself as a raceless artist amounts to a suicide of the self and becomes the obstruction that prevents Cullen from making a fierce and unapologetic contribution to American literature, one steeped in and informed by the living culture of his people. Hughes would certainly have endorsed the aspirations expressed in Johnson's *Book of American Negro Poetry*:

What the colored poet in the United States needs to do is something like what Synge did for the Irish; he needs to find a form that will express the racial spirit by symbols from within rather than by symbols from without, . . . a form expressing the imagery, the idioms, the peculiar turns of thought, and the distinctive humor and pathos, too, of the Negro, but which will also be capable of voicing the deepest and highest emotions and aspirations, and allow of the widest range of subjects and the widest scope of treatment.

He looked forward—in "The Negro Artist and the Racial Mountain"—to a time when race would leave free expression unobstructed:

The younger Negro artists who create now intend to express our individual dark-skinned selves without fear or shame. If white people are pleased we are glad. If they are not, it doesn't matter. We know we are beautiful. And ugly, too. The tom-tom cries, and the tom-tom laughs. If colored people are pleased we are glad. If they are not, their displeasure doesn't matter either. We build our temples for tomorrow, strong as we know how, and we stand on top of the mountain free within ourselves.

If Hughes and Cullen were competitors, of sorts, for the prize of principal African American poet of their generation, Cullen may have had an early lead, and during the later 1920s and early 1930s they were often discussed in tandem. Over time, Hughes has arguably become the more canonical of the two (even as a handful of Cullen's poems continue to be widely anthologized and read); his openness to modernism gave him an edge, as did his exploration and embrace of African American folk traditions. Hughes ultimately expanded the range of possibilities and set new standards for what African American poetry and indeed any poetry could sound like. Cullen, in his way, can sometimes sound like Edna St. Vincent Millay, whom he admired immensely: not only "white," if one must, but even whiter, and even as race was his frequent theme. Hughes's reservations about what might be called the defensive propriety of Cullen's diction have to some extent stuck in the reception history of Harlem Renaissance poetry. As black writers during the Harlem Renaissance and the remainder of the twentieth century increasingly explored the literary possibilities of black vernaculars, Cullen's work came to seem a less vital part of African American tradition, an impressive but unproductive cul-de-sac.

Cullen could not have been unaware of the aspersions Hughes had cast on his work. Indeed, his poem "To Certain Critics"—included in his book *The Black Christ* (1929)—offers a pointed response. Cullen's locution ("certain critics") leaves Hughes unnamed, just as Hughes avoided naming Cullen—the poet who secretly wished to be white—in "The Negro Artist and the Racial Mountain." But while Cullen's poem is open to broader interpretations, Hughes would certainly be a plausible addressee:

> Then call me traitor if you must,
> Shout treason and default!
> Say I betray a sacred trust
> Aching beyond this vault.
> I'll bear your censure as your praise,
> For never shall the clan
> Confine my singing to its ways
> Beyond the ways of man.

No racial option narrows grief,
Pain is no patriot,
And sorrow plaits her dismal leaf
For all as lief as not.
With blind sheep groping every hill,
Searching an oriflamme,
How shall the shepherd heart then thrill
To only the darker lamb?

Called a "traitor" to his race, Cullen asserts the common, transcendent, human relevance of his themes. Grief, pain, and sorrow belong to all. And with a forceful pun, he pushes back and shames the faction—"the clan"—that would limit his artistic freedom on racial grounds.

* * *

All of these debates around the "racial mountain"—as essential as they are and as ongoing as many of the issues are—can seem claustrophobic and distorting, from the perspective of over eighty-six years later. They have the effect of encouraging us to neglect whole landscapes of poetry *not* notably or necessarily overdetermined by the turbulent long foreground of African American history, or to read too narrowly. I invite the reader to take pleasure, in the pages that follow, in Cullen's many distinctive merits, often little explored or still undiscovered. He is a poet of impudent humor (especially evident in his "Epitaphs"). Later in life—in poems newly published or collected here for the first time—he adopted a stridently political voice that may surprise those already familiar with his poetry, and should dispel the mistaken notion that Cullen, in spite of his occasional claims to the contrary, was "apolitical." Above all, he knows how to hammer the quickness of thought into the turns of form. The astute reader attuned to Cullen's rhetorical gifts will pay special attention to such turning. He is the poet of "Yet" and "But"—of insights that spark *between* his lines as well as in them. He would certainly have understood Ralph Waldo Emerson's edict: "it is not meters, but a meter making argument that makes a poem."

Cullen was addicted to fashioning such arguments, and sought his own brand of freedom in pattern and form. He is as dexterous, in his way, as his "Atlantic City Waiter," from *Color*:

> With subtle poise he grips his tray
> > Of delicate things to eat;
> Choice viands to their mouths half way,
> > The ladies watch his feet
>
> Go carving dexterous avenues
> > Through sly intricacies;
> Ten thousand years on jungle clues
> > Alone shaped feet like these.
>
> For him to be humble who is proud
> > Needs colder artifice;
> Though half his pride is disavowed,
> > In vain the sacrifice.
>
> Sheer through his acquiescent mask
> > Of bland gentility,
> The jungle flames like a copper cask
> > Set where the sun strikes free.

It may help to know that Cullen worked, one summer, as a waiter in Atlantic City; he wrote his friend Langston Hughes from there, complaining about his coworkers but expressing pride in the poems they had inspired. Of course, the "pride" here (self-esteem? animal group? sexual desire?), and the punning "feet," are also Cullen's (throughout? in part?), and this portrait "flames" even brighter as self-portrait. But is it a poem about race? sex? class? poetry? Is it "pagan" or "Christian," and how well reconciled are these tendencies? Like its subject, the poem twists and turns while carrying a complex load, and is a kind of show stopper. But what exactly happens in it? Cullen is simply too "sly," here and elsewhere, to be denigrated as a poet who would "write white" or (on the flip side) be content with mere propaganda in the service of racial uplift. He is a complex and sometimes a real virtuoso performer. Like his waiter on tables, he deserves to be closely watched.

Major Jackson
New York, New York, 2012

Frontispiece to *Color* (second edition, 1928), by Charles Cullen

To You Who Read My Book

Soon every sprinter,
  However fleet,
Comes to a winter
  Of sure defeat:
Though he may race
  Like the hunted doe,
Time has a pace
  To lay him low.

Soon we who sing,
  However high,
Must face the Thing
  We cannot fly.
Yea, though we fling
  Our notes to the sun,
Time will outsing
  Us every one.

All things must change
  As the wind is blown;
Time will estrange
  The flesh from the bone.
The dream shall elude
  The dreamer's clasp,

And only its hood
      Shall comfort his grasp.

A little while,
      Too brief at most,
And even my smile
      Will be a ghost.
A little space,
      A Finger's crook,
And who shall trace
      The path I took?

Who shall declare
      My whereabouts;
Say if in the air
      My being shouts
Along light ways,
      Or if in the sea,
Or deep earth stays
      The germ of me?

Ah, none knows, none,
      Save (but too well)
The Cryptic One
      Who will not tell.

This is my hour
      To wax and climb,
Flaunt a red flower
      In the face of time.
And only an hour
      Time gives, then snap

Goes the flower,
   And dried is the sap.

Juice of the first
   Grapes of my vine,
I proffer your thirst
   My own heart's wine.
Here of my growing
   A red rose sways,
Seed of my sowing,
   And work of my days.

(I run, but time's
   Abreast with me;
I sing, but he climbs
   With my highest C.)

Drink while my blood
   Colors the wine,
Reach while the bud
   Is still on the vine. . . .

Then . . .
   When the hawks of death
Tear at my throat
   Till song and breath
Ebb note by note,
   Turn to this book
Of the mellow word
   For a singing look
At the stricken bird.

Say, "This is the way
He chirped and sung,
    In the sweet heyday
When his heart was young.
    Though his throat is bare,
By death defiled,
    Song labored there
And bore a child."

When the dreadful Ax
    Rives me apart,
When the sharp wedge cracks
    My arid heart,
Turn to this book
    Of the singing me
For a springtime look
    At the wintry tree.

Say, "Thus it was weighed
    With flower and fruit,
Ere the Ax was laid
    Unto its root.
Though the blows fall free
    On a gnarled trunk now,
Once he was a tree
    With a blossomy bough."

COLOR

Yet Do I Marvel

I doubt not God is good, well-meaning, kind,
And did He stoop to quibble could tell why
The little buried mole continues blind,
Why flesh that mirrors Him must some day die,
Make plain the reason tortured Tantalus
Is baited by the fickle fruit, declare
If merely brute caprice dooms Sisyphus
To struggle up a never-ending stair.
Inscrutable His ways are, and immune
To catechism by a mind too strewn
With petty cares to slightly understand
What awful brain compels His awful hand.
Yet do I marvel at this curious thing:
To make a poet black, and bid him sing!

A Song of Praise

(For one who praised his lady's being fair.)

You have not heard my love's dark throat,
    Slow-fluting like a reed,
Release the perfect golden note
    She caged there for my need.

Her walk is like the replica
  Of some barbaric dance
Wherein the soul of Africa
  Is winged with arrogance.

And yet so light she steps across
  The ways her sure feet pass,
She does not dent the smoothest moss
  Or bend the thinnest grass.

My love is dark as yours is fair,
  Yet lovelier I hold her
Than listless maids with pallid hair,
  And blood that's thin and colder.

You-proud-and-to-be-pitied one,
  Gaze on her and despair;
Then seal your lips until the sun
  Discovers one as fair.

Brown Boy to Brown Girl

(*Remembrance on a hill*) (*For Yolande*)

"As surely as I hold your hand in mine,
As surely as your crinkled hair belies
The enamoured sun pretending that he dies
While still he loiters in its glossy shine,
As surely as I break the slender line
That spider linked us with, in no least wise

Am I uncertain that these alien skies
Do not our whole life measure and confine.
No less, once in a land of scarlet suns
And brooding winds, before the hurricane
Bore down upon us, long before this pain,
We found a place where quiet water runs;
I held your hand this way upon a hill,
And felt my heart forebear, my pulse grow still."

A Brown Girl Dead

With two white roses on her breasts,
    White candles at head and feet,
Dark Madonna of the grave she rests;
    Lord Death has found her sweet.

Her mother pawned her wedding ring
    To lay her out in white;
She'd be so proud she'd dance and sing
    To see herself tonight.

To a Brown Girl

(*For Roberta*)

What if his glance is bold and free,
    His mouth the lash of whips?
So should the eyes of lovers be,
    And so a lover's lips.

What if no puritanic strain
    Confines him to the nice?
He will not pass this way again,
    Nor hunger for you twice.

Since in the end consort together
    Magdalen and Mary,
Youth is the time for careless weather:
    Later, lass, be wary.

To a Brown Boy

That brown girl's swagger gives a twitch
    To beauty like a queen;
Lad, never dam your body's itch
    When loveliness is seen.

For there is ample room for bliss
    In pride in clean, brown limbs,
And lips know better how to kiss
    Than how to raise white hymns.

And when your body's death gives birth
    To soil for spring to crown,
Men will not ask if that rare earth
    Was white flesh once, or brown.

Black Magdalens

These have no Christ to spit and stoop
   To write upon the sand,
Inviting him that has not sinned
   To raise the first rude hand.

And if he came they could not buy
   Rich ointment for his feet,
The body's sale scarce yields enough
   To let the body eat.

The chaste clean ladies pass them by
   And draw their skirts aside,
But Magdalens have a ready laugh;
   They wrap their wounds in pride.

They fare full ill since Christ forsook
   The cross to mount a throne,
And Virtue still is stooping down
   To cast the first hard stone.

Atlantic City Waiter

With subtle poise he grips his tray
   Of delicate things to eat;
Choice viands to their mouths half way,
   The ladies watch his feet

Go carving dexterous avenues
    Through sly intricacies;
Ten thousand years on jungle clues
    Alone shaped feet like these.

For him to be humble who is proud
    Needs colder artifice;
Though half his pride is disavowed,
    In vain the sacrifice.

Sheer through his acquiescent mask
    Of bland gentility,
The jungle flames like a copper cask
    Set where the sun strikes free.

Near White

Ambiguous of race they stand,
    By one disowned, scorned of another,
Not knowing where to stretch a hand,
    And cry, "My sister" or "My brother."

Tableau

(*For Donald Duff*)

Locked arm in arm they cross the way,
   The black boy and the white,
The golden splendor of the day,
   The sable pride of night.

From lowered blinds the dark folk stare,
   And here the fair folk talk,
Indignant that these two should dare
   In unison to walk.

Oblivious to look and word
   They pass, and see no wonder
That lightning brilliant as a sword
   Should blaze the path of thunder.

Harlem Wine

This is not water running here,
   These thick rebellious streams
That hurtle flesh and bone past fear
   Down alleyways of dreams.

This is a wine that must flow on
   Not caring how nor where,
So it has ways to flow upon
   Where song is in the air.

So it can woo an artful flute
    With loose, elastic lips,
Its measurement of joy compute
    With blithe, ecstatic hips.

Simon the Cyrenian Speaks

He never spoke a word to me,
    And yet He called my name;
He never gave a sign to me,
    And yet I knew and came.

At first I said, "I will not bear
    His cross upon my back;
He only seeks to place it there
    Because my skin is black."

But He was dying for a dream,
    And He was very meek,
And in His eyes there shone a gleam
    Men journey far to seek.

It was Himself my pity bought;
    I did for Christ alone
What all of Rome could not have wrought
    With bruise of lash or stone.

Incident

(*For Eric Walrond*)

Once riding in old Baltimore,
   Heart-filled, head-filled with glee,
I saw a Baltimorean
   Keep looking straight at me.

Now I was eight and very small,
   And he was no whit bigger,
And so I smiled, but he poked out
   His tongue, and called me, "Nigger."

I saw the whole of Baltimore
   From May until December;
Of all the things that happened there
   That's all that I remember.

Two Who Crossed a Line

(*She Crosses*)

From where she stood the air she craved
   Smote with the smell of pine;
It was too much to bear; she braved
   Her gods and crossed the line.

And we were hurt to see her go,
   With her fair face and hair,
And veins too thin and blue to show
   What mingled blood flowed there.

We envied her a while, who still
    Pursued the hated track;
Then we forgot her name, until
    One day her shade came back.

Calm as a wave without a crest,
    Sorrow-proud and sorrow-wise,
With trouble sucking at her breast,
    With tear-disdainful eyes,

She slipped into her ancient place,
    And, no word asked, gave none;
Only the silence in her face
    Said seats were dear in the sun.

Two Who Crossed a Line

(*He Crosses*)

He rode across like a cavalier,
    Spurs clicking hard and loud;
And where he tarried dropped his tear
    On heads he left low-bowed.

But, "Even Stephen," he cried, and struck
    His steed an urgent blow;
He swore by youth he was a buck
    With savage oats to sow.

To even up some standing scores,
    From every flower bed
He passed, he plucked by threes and fours
    Till wheels whirled in his head.

But long before the drug could tell,
    He took his anodyne;
With scornful grace, he bowed farewell
    And retraversed the line.

Saturday's Child

Some are teethed on a silver spoon,
    With the stars strung for a rattle;
I cut my teeth as the black raccoon—
    For implements of battle.

Some are swaddled in silk and down,
    And heralded by a star;
They swathed my limbs in a sackcloth gown
    On a night that was black as tar.

For some, godfather and goddame
    The opulent fairies be;
Dame Poverty gave me my name,
    And Pain godfathered me.

For I was born on Saturday—
   "Bad time for planting a seed,"
Was all my father had to say,
   And, "One mouth more to feed."

Death cut the strings that gave me life,
   And handed me to Sorrow,
The only kind of middle wife
   My folks could beg or borrow.

The Dance of Love

(*After reading René Maran's "Batouala"*)

All night we danced upon our windy hill,
Your dress a cloud of tangled midnight hair,
And love was much too much for me to wear
My leaves; the killer roared above his kill,
But you danced on, and when some star would spill
Its red and white upon you whirling there,
I sensed a hidden beauty in the air;
Though you danced on, my heart and I stood still.

But suddenly a bit of morning crept
Along your trembling sides of ebony;
I saw the tears your tired limbs had wept,
And how your breasts heaved high, how languidly
Your dark arms moved; I drew you close to me;
We flung ourselves upon our hill and slept.

Pagan Prayer

Not for myself I make this prayer,
    But for this race of mine
That stretches forth from shadowed places
    Dark hands for bread and wine.

For me, my heart is pagan mad,
    My feet are never still,
But give them hearths to keep them warm
    In homes high on a hill.

For me, my faith lies fallowing,
    I bow not till I see,
But these are humble and believe;
    Bless their credulity.

For me, I pay my debts in kind,
    And see no better way,
Bless these who turn the other cheek
    For love of you, and pray.

Our Father, God, our Brother, Christ—
    So are we taught to pray;
Their kinship seems a little thing
    Who sorrow all the day.

Our Father, God; our Brother, Christ,
    Or are we bastard kin,
That to our plaints your ears are closed,
    Your doors barred from within?

Our Father, God; our Brother, Christ,
    Retrieve my race again;
So shall you compass this black sheep,
    This pagan heart. Amen.

Wisdom Cometh With the Years

Now I am young and credulous,
    My heart is quick to bleed
At courage in the tremulous
    Slow sprouting of a seed.

Now I am young and sensitive,
    Man's lack can stab me through;
I own no stitch I would not give
    To him that asked me to.

Now I am young and a fool for love,
    My blood goes mad to see
A brown girl pass me like a dove
    That flies melodiously.

Let me be lavish of my tears,
    And dream that false is true;
Though wisdom cometh with the years,
    The barren days come, too.

To My Fairer Brethren

Though I score you with my best,
  Treble circumstance
Must confirm the verdict, lest
  It be laid to chance.

Insufficient that I match you
  Every coin you flip;
Your demand is that I catch you
  Squarely on the hip.

Should I wear my wreaths a bit
  Rakishly and proud,
I have bought my right to it;
  Let it be allowed.

Fruit of the Flower

My father is a quiet man
  With sober, steady ways;
For simile, a folded fan;
  His nights are like his days.

My mother's life is puritan,
  No hint of cavalier,
A pool so calm you're sure it can
  Have little depth to fear.

And yet my father's eyes can boast
    How full his life has been;
There haunts them yet the languid ghost
    Of some still sacred sin.

And though my mother chants of God,
    And of the mystic river,
I've seen a bit of checkered sod
    Set all her flesh aquiver.

Why should he deem it pure mischance
    A son of his is fain
To do a naked tribal dance
    Each time he hears the rain?

Why should she think it devil's art
    That all my songs should be
Of love and lovers, broken heart,
    And wild sweet agony?

Who plants a seed begets a bud,
    Extract of that same root;
Why marvel at the hectic blood
    That flushes this wild fruit?

The Shroud of Color

(*For Llewellyn Ransom*)

"Lord, being dark," I said, "I cannot bear
The further touch of earth, the scented air;
Lord, being dark, forewilled to that despair
My color shrouds me in, I am as dirt
Beneath my brother's heel; there is a hurt
In all the simple joys which to a child
Are sweet; they are contaminate, defiled
By truths of wrongs the childish vision fails
To see; too great a cost this birth entails.
I strangle in this yoke drawn tighter than
The worth of bearing it, just to be man.
I am not brave enough to pay the price
In full; I lack the strength to sacrifice.
I who have burned my hands upon a star,
And climbed high hills at dawn to view the far
Illimitable wonderments of earth,
For whom all cups have dripped the wine of mirth,
For whom the sea has strained her honeyed throat
Till all the world was sea, and I a boat
Unmoored, on what strange quest I willed to float;
Who wore a many-colored coat of dreams,
Thy gift, O Lord—I whom sun-dabbled streams
Have washed, whose bare brown thighs have held the sun
Incarcerate until his course was run,
I who considered man a high-perfected
Glass where loveliness could lie reflected,
Now that I sway athwart Truth's deep abyss,
Denuding man for what he was and is,

Shall breath and being so inveigle me
That I can damn my dreams to hell, and be
Content, each new-born day, anew to see
The steaming crimson vintage of my youth
Incarnadine the altar-slab of Truth?

Or hast Thou, Lord, somewhere I cannot see,
A lamb imprisoned in a bush for me?

Not so? Then let me render one by one
Thy gifts, while still they shine; some little sun
Yet gilds these thighs; my coat, albeit worn,
Still holds its colors fast; albeit torn,
My heart will laugh a little yet, if I
May win of Thee this grace, Lord: on this high
And sacrificial hill 'twixt earth and sky,
To dream still pure all that I loved, and die.
There is no other way to keep secure
My wild chimeras; grave-locked against the lure
Of Truth, the small hard teeth of worms, yet less
Envenomed than the mouth of Truth, will bless
Them into dust and happy nothingness.
Lord, Thou art God; and I, Lord, what am I
But dust? With dust my place. Lord, let me die."

Across the earth's warm, palpitating crust
I flung my body in embrace; I thrust
My mouth into the grass and sucked the dew,
Then gave it back in tears my anguish drew;
So hard I pressed against the ground, I felt
The smallest sandgrain like a knife, and smelt

The next year's flowering; all this to speed
My body's dissolution, fain to feed
The worms. And so I groaned, and spent my strength
Until, all passion spent, I lay full length
And quivered like a flayed and bleeding thing.

So lay till lifted on a great black wing
That had no mate nor flesh-apparent trunk
To hamper it; with me all time had sunk
Into oblivion; when I awoke
The wing hung poised above two cliffs that broke
The bowels of the earth in twain, and cleft
The seas apart. Below, above, to left,
To right, I saw what no man saw before:
Earth, hell, and heaven; sinew, vein, and core.
All things that swim or walk or creep or fly,
All things that live and hunger, faint and die,
Were made majestic then and magnified
By sight so clearly purged and deified.
The smallest bug that crawls was taller than
A tree, the mustard seed loomed like a man.
The earth that writhes eternally with pain
Of birth, and woe of taking back her slain,
Laid bare her teeming bosom to my sight,
And all was struggle, gasping breath, and fight.
A blind worm here dug tunnels to the light,
And there a seed, racked with heroic pain,
Thrust eager tentacles to sun and rain;
It climbed; it died; the old love conquered me
To weep the blossom it would never be.
But here a bud won light; it burst and flowered

Into a rose whose beauty challenged, "Coward!"
There was no thing alive save only I
That held life in contempt and longed to die.
And still I writhed and moaned, "The curse, the curse,
Than animated death, can death be worse?"

"Dark child of sorrow, mine no less, what art
Of mine can make thee see and play thy part?
The key to all strange things is in thy heart."

What voice was this that coursed like liquid fire
Along my flesh, and turned my hair to wire?

I raised my burning eyes, beheld a field
All multitudinous with carnal yield,
A grim ensanguined mead whereon I saw
Evolve the ancient fundamental law
Of tooth and talon, fist and nail and claw.
There with the force of living, hostile hills
Whose clash the hemmed-in vale with clamor fills,
With greater din contended fierce majestic wills
Of beast with beast, of man with man, in strife
For love of what my heart despised, for life
That unto me at dawn was now a prayer
For night, at night a bloody heart-wrung tear
For day again; for *this*, these groans
From tangled flesh and interlockèd bones.
And no thing died that did not give
A testimony that it longed to live.
Man, strange composite blend of brute and god,
Pushed on, nor backward glanced where last he trod.

He seemed to mount a misty ladder flung
Pendant from a cloud, yet never gained a rung
But at his feet another tugged and clung.
My heart was still a pool of bitterness,
Would yield nought else, nought else confess.
I spoke (although no form was there
To see, I knew an ear was there to hear),
"Well, let them fight; they *can* whose flesh is fair."

Crisp lightning flashed; a wave of thunder shook
My wing; a pause, and then a speaking, "Look."

I scarce dared trust my ears or eyes for awe
Of what they heard, and dread of what they saw;
For, privileged beyond degree, this flesh
Beheld God and His heaven in the mesh
Of Lucifer's revolt, saw Lucifer
Glow like the sun, and like a dulcimer
I heard his sin-sweet voice break on the yell
Of God's great warriors: Gabriel,
Saint Clair and Michael, Israfel and Raphael.
And strange it was to see God with His back
Against a wall, to see Christ hew and hack
Till Lucifer, pressed by the mighty pair,
And losing inch by inch, clawed at the air
With fevered wings; then, lost beyond repair,
He tricked a mass of stars into his hair;
He filled his hands with stars, crying as he fell,
"A star's a star although it burns in hell."
So God was left to His divinity,
Omnipotent at that most costly fee.

There was a lesson here, but still the clod
In me was sycophant unto the rod,
And cried, "Why mock me thus? Am I a god?"

"One trial more: this failing, then I give
You leave to die; no further need to live."

Now suddenly a strange wild music smote
A chord long impotent in me; a note
Of jungles, primitive and subtle, throbbed
Against my echoing breast, and tom-toms sobbed
In every pulse-beat of my frame. The din
A hollow log bound with a python's skin
Can make wrought every nerve to ecstasy,
And I was wind and sky again, and sea,
And all sweet things that flourish, being free.

Till all at once the music changed its key.

And now it was of bitterness and death,
The cry the lash extorts, the broken breath
Of liberty enchained; and yet there ran
Through all a harmony of faith in man,
A knowledge all would end as it began.
All sights and sounds and aspects of my race
Accompanied this melody, kept pace
With it; with music all their hopes and hates
Were charged, not to be downed by all the fates.
And somehow it was borne upon my brain
How being dark, and living through the pain
Of it, is courage more than angels have. I knew

What storms and tumults lashed the tree that grew
This body that I was, this cringing I
That feared to contemplate a changing sky,
This I that grovelled, whining, "Let me die,"
While others struggled in Life's abattoir.
The cries of all dark people near or far
Were billowed over me, a mighty surge
Of suffering in which my puny grief must merge
And lose itself; I had no further claim to urge
For death; in shame I raised my dust-grimed head,
And though my lips moved not, God knew I said,
"Lord, not for what I saw in flesh or bone
Of fairer men; not raised on faith alone;
Lord, I will live persuaded by mine own.
I cannot play the recreant to these;
My spirit has come home, that sailed the doubtful
        seas."
With the whiz of a sword that severs space,
The wing dropped down at a dizzy pace,
And flung me on my hill flat on my face;
Flat on my face I lay defying pain,
Glad of the blood in my smallest vein,
And in my hands I clutched a loyal dream,
Still spitting fire, bright twist and coil and gleam,
And chiselled like a hound's white tooth.
"Oh, I will match you yet," I cried, "to truth."

Right glad I was to stoop to what I once had spurned,
Glad even unto tears; I laughed aloud; I turned
Upon my back, and though the tears for joy would run,
My sight was clear; I looked and saw the rising sun.

Heritage

(*For Harold Jackman*)

What is Africa to me:
Copper sun or scarlet sea,
Jungle star or jungle track,
Strong bronzed men, or regal black
Women from whose loins I sprang
When the birds of Eden sang?
One three centuries removed
From the scenes his fathers loved,
Spicy grove, cinnamon tree,
What is Africa to me?

So I lie, who all day long
Want no sound except the song
Sung by wild barbaric birds
Goading massive jungle herds,
Juggernauts of flesh that pass
Trampling tall defiant grass
Where young forest lovers lie,
Plighting troth beneath the sky.
So I lie, who always hear,
Though I cram against my ear
Both my thumbs, and keep them there,
Great drums throbbing through the air.
So I lie, whose fount of pride,
Dear distress, and joy allied,
Is my somber flesh and skin,
With the dark blood dammed within
Like great pulsing tides of wine

That, I fear, must burst the fine
Channels of the chafing net
Where they surge and foam and fret.

Africa? A book one thumbs
Listlessly, till slumber comes.
Unremembered are her bats
Circling through the night, her cats
Crouching in the river reeds,
Stalking gentle flesh that feeds
By the river brink; no more
Does the bugle-throated roar
Cry that monarch claws have leapt
From the scabbards where they slept.
Silver snakes that once a year
Doff the lovely coats you wear,
Seek no covert in your fear
Lest a mortal eye should see;
What's your nakedness to me?
Here no leprous flowers rear
Fierce corollas in the air;
Here no bodies sleek and wet,
Dripping mingled rain and sweat,
Tread the savage measures of
Jungle boys and girls in love.
What is last year's snow to me,
Last year's anything? The tree
Budding yearly must forget
How its past arose or set—
Bough and blossom, flower, fruit,
Even what shy bird with mute

Wonder at her travail there,
Meekly labored in its hair.
One three centuries removed
From the scenes his fathers loved,
Spicy grove, cinnamon tree,
What is Africa to me?

So I lie, who find no peace
Night or day, no slight release
From the unremittent beat
Made by cruel padded feet
Walking through my body's street.
Up and down they go, and back,
Treading out a jungle track.
So I lie, who never quite
Safely sleep from rain at night—
I can never rest at all
When the rain begins to fall;
Like a soul gone mad with pain
I must match its weird refrain;
Ever must I twist and squirm,
Writhing like a baited worm,
While its primal measures drip
Through my body, crying, "Strip!
Doff this new exuberance.
Come and dance the Lover's Dance!"
In an old remembered way
Rain works on me night and day.

Quaint, outlandish heathen gods
Black men fashion out of rods,

Clay, and brittle bits of stone,
In a likeness like their own,
My conversion came high-priced;
I belong to Jesus Christ,
Preacher of humility;
Heathen gods are naught to me.

Father, Son, and Holy Ghost,
So I make an idle boast;
Jesus of the twice-turned cheek,
Lamb of God, although I speak
With my mouth thus, in my heart
Do I play a double part.
Ever at Thy glowing altar
Must my heart grow sick and falter,
Wishing He I served were black,
Thinking then it would not lack
Precedent of pain to guide it,
Let who would or might deride it;
Surely then this flesh would know
Yours had borne a kindred woe.
Lord, I fashion dark gods, too,
Daring even to give You
Dark despairing features where,
Crowned with dark rebellious hair,
Patience wavers just so much as
Mortal grief compels, while touches
Quick and hot, of anger, rise
To smitten cheek and weary eyes.
Lord, forgive me if my need
Sometimes shapes a human creed.

All day long and all night through,
One thing only must I do:
Quench my pride and cool my blood,
Lest I perish in the flood.
Lest a hidden ember set
Timber that I thought was wet
Burning like the dryest flax,
Melting like the merest wax,
Lest the grave restore its dead.
Not yet has my heart or head
In the least way realized
They and I are civilized.

EPITAPHS

For a Poet

I have wrapped my dreams in a silken cloth,
And laid them away in a box of gold;
Where long will cling the lips of the moth,
I have wrapped my dreams in a silken cloth;
I hide no hate; I am not even wroth
Who found earth's breath so keen and cold;
I have wrapped my dreams in a silken cloth,
And laid them away in a box of gold.

For My Grandmother

This lovely flower fell to seed;
   Work gently, sun and rain;
She held it as her dying creed
   That she would grow again.

For a Cynic

Birth is a crime
All men commit;
Life gives them time
To atone for it;
Death ends the rhyme
As the price for it.

For a Singer

Death clogged this flute
   At its highest note;
Song sleeps here mute
   In this breathless throat.

For a Virgin

For forty years I shunned the lust
   Inherent in my clay;
Death only was so amorous
   I let him have his way.

For a Lady I Know

She even thinks that up in heaven
    Her class lies late and snores,
While poor black cherubs rise at seven
    To do celestial chores.

For a Lovely Lady

A creature slender as a reed,
    And sad-eyed as a doe
Lies here (but take my word for it,
    And do not pry below).

For an Atheist

Mountains cover me like rain,
Billows whirl and rise;
Hide me from the stabbing pain
In His reproachful eyes.

For an Evolutionist and His Opponent

Showing that our ways agreed,
   Death is proof enough;
Body seeks the primal clay,
   Soul transcends the slough.

For an Anarchist

What matters that I stormed and swore?
   Not Samson with an ass's jaw,
Not though a forest of hair he wore,
   Could break death's adamantine law.

For a Magician

I whose magic could explore
   Ways others might not guess or see,
Now am barred behind a door
   That has no "Open Sesame."

For a Pessimist

He wore his coffin for a hat,
   Calamity his cape,
While on his face a death's-head sat
   And waved a bit of crape.

For a Mouthy Woman

God and the devil still are wrangling
    Which should have her, which repel;
God wants no discord in his heaven;
    Satan has enough in hell.

For a Philosopher

Here lies one who tried to solve
    The riddle of being and breath:
The wee blind mole that gnaws his bones
    Tells him the answer is death.

For an Unsuccessful Sinner

I boasted my sins were sure to sink me
    Out of all sound and sight of glory;
And the most I've won for all my pains
    Is a century of purgatory.

For a Fool

On earth the wise man makes the rules,
    And is the fool's adviser,
But here the wise are as the fools,
    (And no man is the wiser).

For One Who Gayly Sowed His Oats

My days were a thing for me to live,
    For others to deplore;
I took of life all it could give:
    Rind, inner fruit, and core.

For a Skeptic

Blood-brother unto Thomas whose
    Weak faith doubt kept in trammels,
His little credence strained at gnats—
    But grew robust on camels.

For a Fatalist

Life ushers some as heirs-elect
    To weather wind and gale;
Here lies a man whose ships were wrecked
    Ere he could hoist a sail.

For Daughters of Magdalen

Ours is the ancient story:
    Delicate flowers of sin,
Lilies, arrayed in glory,
    That would not toil nor spin.

For a Wanton

To men no more than so much cover
    For them to doff or try,
I found in Death a constant lover:
    Here in his arms I lie.

For a Preacher

Vanity of vanities,
    All is vanity; yea,
Even the rod He flayed you with
    Crumbled and turned to clay.

For One Who Died Singing of Death

He whose might you sang so well
    Living, will not let you rust:
Death has set the golden bell
    Pealing in the courts of dust.

For John Keats, Apostle of Beauty

Not writ in water, nor in mist,
    Sweet lyric throat, thy name;
Thy singing lips that cold death kissed
    Have seared his own with flame.

For Hazel Hall, American Poet

Soul-troubled at the febrile ways of breath,
   Her timid breast shot through with faint alarm,
"Yes, I'm a stranger here," she said to Death,
   "It's kind of you to let me take your arm."

For Paul Laurence Dunbar

Born of the sorrowful of heart,
   Mirth was a crown upon his head;
Pride kept his twisted lips apart
   In jest, to hide a heart that bled.

For Joseph Conrad

Not of the dust, but of the wave
His final couch should be;
They lie not easy in a grave
Who once have known the sea.
How shall earth's meagre bed enthrall
The hardiest seaman of them all?

For Myself

What's in this grave is worth your tear;
    There's more than the eye can see;
Folly and Pride and Love lie here
    Buried alive with me.

All the Dead

Priest and layman, virgin, strumpet,
    Good and ill commingled sleep,
Waiting till the dreadful trumpet
    Separates the wolves and sheep.

FOR LOVE'S SAKE

Oh, for a Little While Be Kind
(For Ruth Marie)

Oh, for a little while be kind to me
Who stand in such imperious need of you,
And for a fitful space let my head lie
Happily on your passion's frigid breast.
Although yourself no more resigned to me
Than on all bitter yesterdays I knew,
This half a loaf from sumptuous crumbs your shy
Reneging hand lets fall shall make me blest.
The sturdy homage of a love that throws
Its strength about you, dawn and dusk, at bed
And board, is not for scorn. When all is said
With final amen certitude, who knows
But Dives found a matchless fragrance fled
When Lazarus no longer shocked his nose?

If You Should Go

Love, leave me like the light,
    The gently passing day;
We would not know, but for the night,
    When it has slipped away.

Sacrament

She gave her body for my meat,
    Her soul to be my wine,
And prayed that I be made complete
    In sunlight and starshine.

With such abandoned grace she gave
    Of all that passion taught her,
She never knew her tidal wave
    Cast bread on stagnant water.

Bread and Wine

From death of star to new star's birth,
    This ache of limb, this throb of head,
This sweaty shop, this smell of earth,
    For this we pray, "Give daily bread."

Then tenuous with dreams the night,
    The feel of soft brown hands in mine,
Strength from your lips for one more fight:
    Bread's not so dry when dipped in wine.

Spring Reminiscence

"My sweet," you sang, and, "Sweet," I sang,
   And sweet we sang together,
Glad to be young as the world was young,
   Two colts too strong for a tether.

Shall ever a spring be like that spring,
   Or apple blossoms as white;
Or ever clover smell like the clover
   We lay upon that night?

Shall ever your hand lie in my hand,
   Pulsing to it, I wonder;
Or have the gods, being jealous gods,
   Envied us our thunder?

VARIA

Suicide Chant

I am the seed
  The Sower sowed;
I am the deed
  His hand bestowed
Upon the world.

Censure me not
  If a rank weed flood
The garden plot,
  Instead of a bud
To be unfurled.

Bridle your blame
  If the deed prove less
Than the bruited fame
  With which it came
From nothingness.

The seed of a weed
  Cannot be flowered,
Nor a hero's deed
  Spring from a coward.

Pull up the weed;
 Bring plow and mower;
Then fetch new seed
 For the hand of the Sower.

She of the Dancing Feet Sings

(*To Ottie Graham*)

"And what would I do in heaven, pray,
 Me with my dancing feet,
And limbs like apple boughs that sway
 When the gusty rain winds beat?

And how would I thrive in a perfect place
 Where dancing would be sin,
With not a man to love my face,
 Nor an arm to hold me in?

The seraphs and the cherubim
 Would be too proud to bend
To sing the faery tunes that brim
 My heart from end to end.

The wistful angels down in hell
 Will smile to see my face,
And understand, because they fell
 From that all-perfect place."

Judas Iscariot

I think when Judas' mother heard
    His first faint cry the night
That he was born, that worship stirred
    Her at the sound and sight.
She thought his was as fair a frame
    As flesh and blood had worn;
I think she made this lovely name
    For him—"Star of my morn."

As any mother's son he grew
    From spring to crimson spring;
I think his eyes were black, or blue,
    His hair curled like a ring.
His mother's heart-strings were a lute
    Whereon he all day played;
She listened rapt, abandoned, mute,
    To every note he made.

I think he knew the growing Christ,
    And played with Mary's son,
And where mere mortal craft sufficed,
    There Judas may have won.
Perhaps he little cared or knew,
    So folly-wise is youth,
That He whose hand his hand clung to
    Was flesh-embodied Truth;

Until one day he heard young Christ,
    With far-off eyes agleam,

Tell of a mystic, solemn tryst
    Between Him and a dream.
And Judas listened, wonder-eyed,
    Until the Christ was through,
Then said, "And I, though good betide,
    Or ill, will go with you."

And so he followed, heard Christ preach,
    Saw how by miracle
The blind man saw, the dumb got speech,
    The leper found him well.
And Judas in those holy hours
    Loved Christ, and loved Him much,
And in his heart he sensed dead flowers
    Bloom at the Master's touch.

And when Christ felt the death hour creep
    With sullen, drunken lurch,
He said to Peter, "Feed my sheep,
    And build my holy church."
He gave to each the special task
    That should be his to do,
But reaching one, I hear him ask,
    "What shall I give to you?"

Then Judas in his hot desire
    Said, "Give me what you will."
Christ spoke to him with words of fire,
    "Then, Judas, you must kill
One whom you love, One who loves you
    As only God's son can:

This is the work for you to do
    To save the creature man."

"And men to come will curse your name,
    And hold you up to scorn;
In all the world will be no shame
    Like yours; this is love's thorn.
It takes strong will of heart and soul,
    But man is under ban.
Think, Judas, can you play this role
    In heaven's mystic plan?"

So Judas took the sorry part,
    Went out and spoke the word,
And gave the kiss that broke his heart,
    But no one knew or heard.
And no one knew what poison ate
    Into his palm that day,
Where, bright and damned, the monstrous weight
    Of thirty white coins lay.

It was not death that Judas found
    Upon a kindly tree;
The man was dead long ere he bound
    His throat as final fee.
And who can say if on that day
    When gates of pearl swung wide,
Christ did not go His honored way
    With Judas by His side?

I think somewhere a table round
   Owns Jesus as its head,
And there the saintly twelve are found
   Who followed where He led.
And Judas sits down with the rest,
   And none shrinks from His hand,
For there the worst is as the best,
   And there they understand.

And you may think of Judas, friend,
   As one who broke his word,
Whose neck came to a bitter end
   For giving up his Lord.
But I would rather think of him
   As the little Jewish lad
Who gave young Christ heart, soul, and limb,
   And all the love he had.

The Wise

(*For Alain Locke*)

Dead men are wisest, for they know
How far the roots of flowers go,
How long a seed must rot to grow.

Dead men alone bear frost and rain
On throbless heart and heatless brain,
And feel no stir of joy or pain.

Dead men alone are satiate;
They sleep and dream and have no weight,
To curb their rest, of love or hate.

Strange, men should flee their company,
Or think me strange who long to be
Wrapped in their cool immunity.

Mary, Mother of Christ

That night she felt those searching hands
Grip deep upon her breast,
She laughed and sang a silly tune
To lull her babe to rest;

That night she kissed his coral lips
How could she know the rest?

Dialogue

Soul: There is no stronger thing than song;
           In sun and rain and leafy trees
           It wafts the timid soul along
           On crested waves of melodies.

Body: But leaves the body bare to feed
           Its hunger with its very need.

Soul: Although the frenzied belly writhes,
           Yet render up in song your tithes;
           Song is the weakling's oaken rod,
           His Jacob's ladder dropped from God.

Body: Song is not drink; song is not meat,
           Nor strong, thick shoes for naked feet.

Soul: Who sings by unseen hands is fed
           With honeyed milk and warm, white bread;
           His ways in pastures green are led,
           And perfumed oil illumes his head;
           His cup with wine is surfeited,
           And when the last low note is read,
           He sings among the lipless dead
           With singing stars to crown his head.

Body: But will song buy a wooden box
           The length of me from toe to crown,
           To keep me safe from carrion flocks
           When singing's done and lyre laid down?

In Memory of Col. Charles Young

Along the shore the tall, thin grass
   That fringes that dark river,
While sinuously soft feet pass,
   Begins to bleed and quiver.

The great dark voice breaks with a sob
   Across the womb of night;
Above your grave the tom-toms throb,
   And the hills are weird with light.

The great dark heart is like a well
   Drained bitter by the sky,
And all the honeyed lies they tell
   Come there to thirst and die.

No lie is strong enough to kill
   The roots that work below;
From your rich dust and slaughtered will
   A tree with tongues will grow.

To My Friends

You feeble few that hold me somewhat more
Than all I am; base clay and spittle joined
To shape an aimless whim substantial; coined
Amiss one idle hour, this heart, though poor,—
O golden host I count upon the ends

Of one bare hand, with fingers still to spare,—
Is rich enough for this: to harbor there
In opulence its frugal meed of friends.
Let neither lose his faith, lest by such loss
Each find insufferable his daily cross.
And be not less immovable to me,
Not less love-leal and staunch, than my heart is.
In brief, these fine heroics come to this,
My friends: if you are true, I needs must be.

Gods

I fast and pray and go to church,
    And put my penny in,
But God's not fooled by such slight tricks,
    And I'm not saved from sin.

I cannot hide from Him the gods
    That revel in my heart,
Nor can I find an easy word
    To tell them to depart:

God's alabaster turrets gleam
    Too high for me to win,
Unless He turns His face and lets
    Me bring my own gods in.

To John Keats, Poet. At Spring Time*

(*For Carl Van Vechten*)

I cannot hold my peace, John Keats;
There never was a spring like this;
It is an echo, that repeats
My last year's song and next year's bliss.
I know, in spite of all men say
Of Beauty, you have felt her most.
Yea, even in your grave her way
Is laid. Poor, troubled, lyric ghost,
Spring never was so fair and dear
As Beauty makes her seem this year.

I cannot hold my peace, John Keats,
I am as helpless in the toil
Of Spring as any lamb that bleats
To feel the solid earth recoil
Beneath his puny legs. Spring beats
Her tocsin call to those who love her,
And lo! the dogwood petals cover
Her breast with drifts of snow, and sleek
White gulls fly screaming to her, and hover
About her shoulders, and kiss her cheek,
While white and purple lilacs muster
A strength that bears them to a cluster
Of color and odor; for her sake
All things that slept are now awake.

*Spring, 1924

And you and I, shall we lie still,
John Keats, while Beauty summons us?
Somehow I feel your sensitive will
Is pulsing up some tremulous
Sap road of a maple tree, whose leaves
Grow music as they grow, since your
Wild voice is in them, a harp that grieves
For life that opens death's dark door.
Though dust, your fingers still can push
The Vision Splendid to a birth,
Though now they work as grass in the hush
Of the night on the broad sweet page of the earth.

"John Keats is dead," they say, but I
Who hear your full insistent cry
In bud and blossom, leaf and tree,
Know John Keats still writes poetry.
And while my head is earthward bowed
To read new life sprung from your shroud,
Folks seeing me must think it strange
That merely spring should so derange
My mind. They do not know that you,
John Keats, keep revel with me, too.

On Going

(*For Willard Johnson*)

A grave is all too weak a thing
    To hold my fancy long;
I'll bear a blossom with the spring,
    Or be a blackbird's song,

I think that I shall fade with ease,
   Melt into earth like snow,
Be food for hungry, growing trees,
   Or help the lilies blow.

And if my love should lonely walk,
   Quite of my nearness fain,
I may come back to her, and talk
   In liquid words of rain.

Harsh World That Lashest Me

(*For Walter White*)

Harsh World that lashest me each day,
   Dub me not cowardly because
I seem to find no sudden way
   To throttle you or clip your claws.
No force compels me to the wound
   Whereof my body bears the scar;
Although my feet are on the ground,
   Doubt not my eyes are on a star.

You cannot keep me captive, World,
   Entrammeled, chained, spit on, and spurned.
More free than all your flags unfurled,
   I give my body to be burned.
I mount my cross because I will,
   I drink the hemlock which you give
For wine which you withhold—and still,
   Because I will not die, I live.

I live because an ember in
　　Me smoulders to regain its fire,
Because what is and what has been
　　Not yet have conquered my desire.
I live to prove the groping clod
　　Is surely more than simple dust;
I live to see the breath of God
　　Beatify the carnal crust.

But when I will, World, I can go,
　　Though triple bronze should wall me round,
Slip past your guard as swift as snow,
　　Translated without pain or sound.
Within myself is lodged the key
　　To that vast room of couches laid
For those too proud to live and see
　　Their dreams of light eclipsed in shade.

Requiescam

I am for sleeping and forgetting
　　All that has gone before;
I am for lying still and letting
　　Who will beat at my door;
I would my life's cold sun were setting
　　To rise for me no more.

COLOR

From the Dark Tower

(*To Charles S. Johnson*)

We shall not always plant while others reap
The golden increment of bursting fruit,
Not always countenance, abject and mute,
That lesser men should hold their brothers cheap;
Not everlastingly while others sleep
Shall we beguile their limbs with mellow flute,
Not always bend to some more subtle brute;
We were not made eternally to weep.

The night whose sable breast relieves the stark,
White stars is no less lovely being dark,
And there are buds that cannot bloom at all
In light, but crumple, piteous, and fall;
So in the dark we hide the heart that bleeds,
And wait, and tend our agonizing seeds.

Threnody for a Brown Girl

Weep not, you who love her;
What rebellious flow
Grief undams shall recover
Whom the gods bid go?
Sorrow rising like a wall,
Bitter, blasphemous,
What avails it to recall
Beauty back to us?

Think not this grave shall keep her,
This marriage-bed confine;
Death may dig it deep and deeper;
She shall climb it like a vine.
Body that was quick and sentient,
Dear as thought or speech,
Death could not with one trenchant
Blow snatch out of reach.

She is nearer than the word
Wasted on her now,
Nearer than the swaying bird
On its rhythmic bough.
Only were our faith as much
As a mustard seed,
Aching, hungry hands might touch
Her as they touch a reed.

Life who was not loth to trade her
Unto death, has done
Better than he planned, has made her

Wise as Solomon.
Now she knows the Why and Wherefore,
Troublous Whence and Whither,
Why men strive and sweat, and care for
Bays that droop and wither.

All the stars she knows by name,
End and origin thereof,
Knows if love be kin to shame,
If shame be less than love.
What was crooked now is straight,
What was rough is plain;
Grief and sorrow have no weight
Now to cause her pain.

Plain to her why fevered blisters
Made her dark hands run,
While her favored, fairer sisters
Neither wrought nor spun;
Clear to her the hidden reason
Men daily fret and toil,
Staving death off for a season
Till soil return to soil.

One to her are flame and frost;
Silence is her singing lark;
We alone are children, lost,
Crying in the dark.
Varied feature now, and form,
Change has bred upon her;
Crush no bug nor nauseous worm
Lest you tread upon her.

Pluck no flower lest she scream;
Bruise no slender reed,
Lest it prove more than it seem,
Lest she groan and bleed.
More than ever trust your brother,
Read him golden, pure;
It may be she finds no other
House so safe and sure.

Set no poet carving
Rhymes to make her laugh;
Only live hearts starving
Need an epitaph.
Lay upon her no white stone
From a foreign quarry;
Earth and sky be these alone
Her obituary.

Swift as startled fawn or swallow,
Silence all her sound,
She has fled; we cannot follow
Further than this mound.
We who take the beaten track
Trying to appease
Hearts near breaking with their lack,
We need elegies.

Confession

If for a day joy masters me,
Think not my wounds are healed;
Far deeper than the scars you see,
I keep the roots concealed.

They shall bear blossoms with the fall;
I have their word for this,
Who tend my roots with rains of gall,
And suns of prejudice.

Uncle Jim

"White folks is white," says uncle Jim;
"A platitude," I sneer;
And then I tell him so is milk,
And the froth upon his beer.

His heart walled up with bitterness,
He smokes his pungent pipe,
And nods at me as if to say,
"Young fool, you'll soon be ripe!"

I have a friend who eats his heart
Away with grief of mine,
Who drinks my joy as tipplers drain
Deep goblets filled with wine.

I wonder why here at his side,
Face-in-the-grass with him,
My mind should stray the Grecian urn
To muse on uncle Jim.

Colored Blues Singer

Some weep to find the Golden Pear
Feeds maggots at the core,
And some grow cold as ice, and bear
Them prouder than before.

But you go singing like the sea
Whose lover turns to land;
You make your grief a melody
And take it by the hand.

Such songs the mellow-bosomed maids
Of Africa intone
For lovers dead in hidden glades,
Slow rotting flesh and bone.

Such keenings tremble from the kraal,
Where sullen-browed abides
The second wife whose dark tears fail
To draw him to her sides.

Somewhere Jeritza breaks her heart
On symbols Verdi wrote;
You tear the strings of your soul apart,
Blood dripping note by note.

Colors

(*To Leland*)

(Red)

She went to buy a brand new hat,
And she was ugly, black, and fat:
"This red becomes you well," they said,
And perched it high upon her head.
And then they laughed behind her back
To see it glow against the black.
She paid for it with regal mien,
And walked out proud as any queen.

(Black)

1

The play is done, the crowds depart; and see
That twisted tortured thing hung from a tree,
Swart victim of a newer Calvary.

2

Yea, he who helped Christ up Golgotha's track,
That Simon who did *not* deny, was black.

(The Unknown Color)

I've often heard my mother say,
When great winds blew across the day,
And, cuddled close and out of sight,
The young pigs squealed with sudden fright
Like something speared or javelined,
"Poor little pigs, they see the wind."

The Litany of the Dark People

Our flesh that was a battle-ground
Shows now the morning-break;
The ancient deities are downed
For Thy eternal sake.
Now that the past is left behind,
Fling wide Thy garment's hem
To keep us one with Thee in mind,
Thou Christ of Bethlehem.

The thorny wreath may ridge our brow,
The spear may mar our side,
And on white wood from a scented bough
We may be crucified;
Yet no assault the old gods make
Upon our agony
Shall swerve our footsteps from the wake
Of Thine toward Calvary.

And if we hunger now and thirst,
Grant our withholders may,
When heaven's constellations burst
Upon Thy crowning day,
Be fed by us, and given to see
Thy mercy in our eyes,
When Bethlehem and Calvary
Are merged in Paradise.

THE DEEP IN LOVE

Pity the Deep in Love
(*To Fiona*)

Pity the deep in love;
They move as men asleep,
Traveling a narrow way
Precipitous and steep.
Tremulous is the lover's breath
With little moans and sighs;
Heavy are the brimming lids
Upon a lover's eyes.

One Day We Played a Game
(*Yolande: Her Poem*)

One day we lay beneath an apple tree,
Tumultuous with fruit, live with the bee,
And there we played a gay, fantastic game
Of our own making, called Name me a Name.
The grave was liberal, letting us endow
Ourselves with names of lovers who by now
Are dust, but rarer dust for loving high
Than they shall be who let the red flame die. . . .

Crouched sphinx-wise in the grass, you hugged your
    knees,
And called me "Abelard;" I, "Heloise,"
Rejoined, and added thereto, "Melisande;"
Then "Pelleas," I heard, and felt a hand
Slide into mine; joy would not let us speak
Awhile, but only sit there cheek to cheek,
Hand clasping hand. . . . till passion made us bold;
"Tristan," you purred to me. . . . I laughed, "Isolde."
"King Ninus, I," I cried; snared in a kiss
You named yourself my dark Semiramis.
"Queen Guinevere," I sang; you, "Lancelot."
My heart grew big with pride to think you'd not
Cried "Arthur," whom his lovely queen forgot
In loving him whose name you called me by. . . .
We two grew mad with loving then, and I
With whirlpool rapture strained you to my breast;
"First love! First love!" I urged, and "Adam!" blessed
My urgency. My lips grew soft with "Eve,"
And round with ardor purposing to leave
Upon your mouth a lasting seal of bliss. . . .
But midway of our kissing came a hiss
Above us in the apple tree; a sweet
Red apple rolled between us at our feet,
And looking up we saw with glide and dip,
Cold supple coils among the branches slip.
"Eve! Eve!" I cried, "Beware!" Too late. You bit
Half of the fruit away. . . . The rest of it
I took, assuring you with misty eyes,
"Fare each as each, we lose no Paradise."

Timid Lover

I who employ a poet's tongue,
Would tell you how
You are a golden damson hung
Upon a silver bough.

I who adore exotic things
Would shape a sound
To be your name, a word that sings
Until the head goes round.

I who am proud with other folk
Would grow complete
In pride on bitter words you spoke,
And kiss your petalled feet.

But never past the frail intent
My will may flow,
Though gentle looks of yours are bent
Upon me where I go.

So must I, starved for love's delight,
Affect the mute,
When love's divinest acolyte
Extends me holy fruit.

Nocturne

Tell me all things false are true,
Bitter sweet, that fools are wise;
I will not doubt nor question you;
I am in a mood for lies.

Tell me all things ill turn good;
Thew and sinew will be stronger
Thriving on the deadly food
Life proffers for their hunger.

Paint love lovely, if you will;
Be crafty, sly, deceptive;
Here is fertile land to till,
Sun-seeking, rain-receptive.

Hold my hand and lie to me;
I will not ask you How nor Why;
I see death drawing nigh to me
Out of the corner of my eye.

Words to My Love

What if you come
Again and swell
The throat of some
Mute bird;
How shall I tell?

How shall I know
That it is so,
Having heard?

Love, let no trick
Of what's to come
Deceive; the quick
So soon grow dumb;
With wine and bread
Our feast is spread;
Let's leave no crumb.

En Passant

If I was born a liar, lass,
And you were born a jade,
It's just the way things come to pass,
And men and mice are made.

I tell you love is like the dew
That trembles on the grass;
You'd not believe me, speaking true,
That love is wormwood, lass.

You swear no other lips but mine
Have clung like this to yours,
But lass, I know how such strong wine
Draws bees and flies by scores.

I now voluptuously bask
Where Jack tomorrow will,
And while we kiss, I long to ask,
"What girl goes up that hill?"

You love me for the liar I am;
I love the minx you are;
'Tis heaven we must bless or damn
That shaped us on a par.

Variations on a Theme

(*The Loss of Love*)

1

This house where Love a little while abode,
Impoverished completely of him now,
Of every vestige bare, drained like a bough
Wherefrom the all-sustaining sap has flowed
Away, yet bears upon its front bestowed
A cabalistic legend telling how
Love for a meagre space deigned to allow
It summer scent before the winter snowed.
Here rots to ruin a splendor proudly calm,
A skeleton whereof the clean bones wear
Their indigence relieved of any qualm
For purple robes that once were folded there.
The mouldy Coliseum draws upon
Our wonder yet . . . no less Love's Parthenon.

2

All through an empty place I go,
And find her not in any room;
The candles and the lamps I light
Go down before a wind of gloom.

Thick-spraddled lies the dust about,
A fit, sad place to write her name
Or draw her face the way she looked
That legendary night she came.

The old house crumbles bit by bit;
Each day I hear the ominous thud
That says another rent is there
For winds to pierce and storms to flood.

My orchards groan and sag with fruit;
Where, Indian-wise, the bees go round;
I let it rot upon the bough;
I eat what falls upon the ground.

The heavy cows go laboring
In agony with clotted teats;
My hands are slack; my blood is cold;
I marvel that my heart still beats.

I have no will to weep or sing,
No least desire to pray or curse;
The loss of love is a terrible thing;
They lie who say that death is worse.

A Song of Sour Grapes

I wish your body were in the grave,
Deep down as a grave may be,
Or rotting under the deepest wave
That ever ploughed the sea.

I wish I never had seen your face,
Or the sinuous curve of your mouth,
Dear as a straw to a man who drowns
Or rain to a land in drouth.

I would that your mother had never borne
Your father's seed to fruit,
That meadow rats had gnawed his corn
Before it gathered root.

In Memoriam

You were the path I had to take
    To find that all
That lay behind its loops and bends
    Was a bare blank wall.

You were the way my curious hands
    Were doomed to learn
That fire, lovely to the sight,
    To the touch will burn.

That yours was no slight rôle, my dear,
   Be well content;
Not everyone is blessed to be
   Wisdom's instrument.

Lament

Now let all lovely things embark
Upon the sea of mist
With her whose luscious mouth the dark,
Grim troubadour has kissed.

The silver clock that ticked away
Her days, and never knew
Its beats were sword thrusts to the clay
That too much beauty slew.

The pillow favored with her tears
And hallowed by her head;
I shall not even keep my fears,
Now their concern is dead.

But where shall I bury sun and rain,
How mortalise the stars,
How still the half-heard cries of pain
That seared her soul with scars?

In what sea depths shall all the seeds
Of every flower die?
Where shall I scatter the broken reeds,
And how erase the sky?

And where shall I find a hole so deep
No troubled ghost may rise?
There will I put my heart to sleep
Wanting her face and eyes.

If Love Be Staunch

If love be staunch, call mountains brittle;
Love is a thing will live
So long, my dear,—oh, just the little
While water stays in a sieve.

Yea, love is deathless as the day
Whose death the stars reveal;
And love is loyal all the way,
If treachery be leal.

Beyond the shadow of a doubt,
No thing is sweet as love,
But, oh, the bitterness spewed out
Of the heart at the end thereof!

Beyond all cavil or complaint,
Love's ways are double-dyed;
Beneath the surplice of a saint
The cloven hooves are spied.

Whom yesterday love rhymed his sun
Today he names a star;
When the course of another day is run,
What will he say you are?

The Spark

Stamp hard, be sure
We leave no spark
That may allure
This placid dark.
At last we learn
That love is cruel;
Fire will not burn
Lacking fuel.

Here, take your heart,
The whole of it;
I want no part,
No smallest bit.
And this is mine?
You took scant care;
My heart could *shine*;
No glaze was there.

Young lips hold wine
The fair world over;
New heads near mine
Will dent the clover;
We need not pine
Now this is over.

Now love is dead
We might be friends;
'Tis best instead
To say all ends,

And when we meet
Pass quickly by;
Oh, speed your feet,
And so will I.

I know a man
Thought a spark was dead
That flamed and ran
A brighter red,
And burned the roof
Above his head.

Song of the Rejected Lover

With silver bell scarce sounding at the pace,
Slow riding down from courtly Camelot,
Roused from the splendor of her escort's grace,
Queen Guinevere turns cold to Lancelot.

For love of me Elaine has kissed Death's face,
For love of me is grief in Astolat,
While for the warm delight of my embrace
Queen Guinevere turns cold to Lancelot.

Thou slender cruelty and slim distress,
Let each to each forgetful and forgot
Abide; for me, a dream-dark loveliness,
Queen Guinevere turns cold to Lancelot.

To One Who Was Cruel

The wound you gave
Will not abide,
Nor what you crave
Be gratified.

Time with deft finger
Probing far,
Will let linger
No sign or scar.

Only a line like snow,
So faint, so thin,
Folks will not know
A wound has been.

Sonnet to a Scornful Lady

(*To Ruth Marie*)

Like some grim gladiator who has fought
Men loving life as lustily as he,
And with red wounds and blood has dearly bought
A forced reprieve from those who came to see
Him die; a suppliant on gory knees
Like him, lean with my passion's hunger, I
Lay bare the bruises of my heart, with these
Imploring, "Love me, lady, or I die."

But unlike him I hear no populace
Enamoured of a brave bout, crying, "Grace!"
Scorn rules your eyes as silence does your mouth;
No golden sceptre raises me from where
I kneel unfavored finding you still fair
Though both your regal thumbs are pointed south.

The Love Tree

Come, let us plant our love as farmers plant
A seed, and you shall water it with tears,
And I shall weed it with my hands until
They bleed. Perchance this buried love of ours
Will fall on goodly ground and bear a tree
With fruit and flowers; pale lovers chancing here
May pluck and eat, and through their veins a sweet
And languid ardor play, their pulses beat
An unimagined tune, their shy lips meet
And part, and bliss repeat again. And men
Will pilgrimage from far and wide to see
This tree for which we two were crucified,
And, happy in themselves, will never know
'Twas break of heart that made the Love Tree grow.

AT CAMBRIDGE

(*With grateful appreciation to Robert S. Hillyer*)

The Wind Bloweth Where It Listeth

"Live like the wind," he said, "unfettered,
  And love me while you can;
And when you will, and can be bettered,
  Go to the better man.

"For you'll grow weary, maybe, sleeping
  So long a time with me;
Like this there'll be no cause for weeping;
  The wind is always free.

"Go when you please," he would be saying,
  His mouth hard on her own;
That's why she stayed and loved the staying,
  Contented to the bone.

And now he's dust, and he but twenty,—
  Frost that was like a flame;
Her kisses on the head death bent, he
  Gave answer to his name.

And now he's dust and with dust lying
  In sullen arrogance;
Death found it hard, far all his trying,
  To shatter such a lance.

She laid him out as fine as any
      That had a priest and ring;
She never spared a silver penny
      For cost of anything.

Her grief is crowned with his child sucking
      The milk of her distress,
As if his father's hands were plucking
      Her buds of bitterness.

He may grow tall as any other,
      Blest with his father's face,
And yield her strength enough to smother
      What some will call disgrace.

He may be cursed and be concerned
      With thoughts of right and wrong,
And brand with "Shame" these two that burned
      Without the legal thong.

Her man would say they were no rabble
      To love like common clay,—
But Christian tongues are trained to babble
      In such a bitter way.

Still, she's this minted gold to pour her,
      This from her man for a mark:
It was no law that held him for her,
      And moved his feet in the dark.

Thoughts in a Zoo

They in their cruel traps, and we in ours,
Survey each other's rage, and pass the hours
Commiserating each the other's woe,
To mitigate his own pain's fiery glow.
Man could but little proffer in exchange
Save that his cages have a larger range.
That lion with his lordly, untamed heart
Has in some man his human counterpart,
Some lofty soul in dreams and visions wrapped,
But in the stifling flesh securely trapped.
Gaunt eagle whose raw pinions stain the bars
That prison you, so men cry for the stars!
Some delve down like the mole far underground,
(Their nature is to burrow, not to bound),
Some, like the snake, with changeless slothful eye,
Stir not, but sleep and smoulder where they lie.

Who is most wretched, these caged ones, or we,
Caught in a vastness beyond our sight to see?

Two Thoughts of Death

1

When I am dead, it will not be
Much matter of concern to me
Who folds my hands, or combs my hair,
Or, pitying their sightless stare,
Draws down the blinds across my eyes.

I shall not have the least surmise
Which of the many loves I had
Weeps most the passing of her lad.
Not what these give, nor what they keep,
Shall gladden or disturb my sleep,
If only one who never guessed
How every tremor in her breast
Reverberated in my own.
In that last hour come and bend down
To kiss my long-expectant mouth
Still curved, in death, to meet her mouth.

2

I am content to play the martyr,
To wear the dunce cap here at school;
For every tear I shed I'll barter
To Death; I'll be no more a fool
When that pale rider reaches down
His hand to me. He'll beat a crown
From all the aches my shoulders bore,
And I shall lord one regal hour
Illumined in all things before
His sickle spears another flower.
While still his shears snarl through my thread,
Dismembering it strand by strand,
While I hang poised between the dead
And quick, into omniscience fanned,
My mind shall glow with one rich spark
Before it ends in endless dark.
These straining eyes, clairvoyant then,
Shall probe beneath the calloused husk

That hides the better selves of men.
And as my day throbs into dusk,
This heart the world has made to bleed,
While all its red stream deathward flows,
Shall comprehend just why the seed
Must agonize to be the rose.

The Poet Puts His Heart to School

Our love has dwindled down to this:
With proper stress and emphasis
To crown a given exercise;
Those lips, that bearing, those great eyes
I once was wont to praise, I trade
Now for technique and for a grade.
That sun in which I used to bask
Now glorifies a schoolboy's task.
Priest am I now for wisdom's pay,
And half a priest's task is to slay,
Nor raise one far-remembering cry
Though with the slain the slayer die.
Aloft the sacred knife is curved:
The gods of knowledge must be served.

Love's Way

Love is not love demanding all, itself
Withholding aught; love's is the nobler way
Of courtesy, that will not feast aware
That the beloved hungers, nor drink unless
The cup be shared down to the last sweet dregs.
Renunciatory never was the thorn
To crown love with, but *prodigal* and *proud!*
Too proud to rest the debtor of the one
Dear passion most it dotes upon, always
Love rehabilitates unto the end.
So let it be with us; the perfect faith
We each to other swear this moment leaves
Our scales harmonious, neither wanting found
Though weighed in such strict balances. So let
It be with us always. I am too proud
To owe you one caress; you must not drop
Beholden to my favor for one least
Endearing term. Should you reveal some stretch
Of sky to me, let me revive some note
Of music lost to you. This is love's way,
That where a heart is asked gives back a heart.

Portrait of a Lover

Weary, restless, now fever's minion, furnace-hot,
Now without reason shivering prey to some great dread;
Trusting, doubting, prone to reveal, yet wishing not
To name this malady whereby his wits are led,

Trapped in this labyrinth without a magic thread,
He gropes bewildered in a most familiar place;
It should be spring by all the signs and portents spread,
But four strong seasons wrangle on this lover's face.

Of all men born he deems himself so much accurst,
His plight so piteous, his proper pain so rare,
The very bread he eats so dry, so fierce his thirst,
What shall we liken such a martyr to? Compare
Him to a man with poison raging in his throat,
And far away the one mind with an antidote.

An Old Story

"I must be ready when he comes," she said,
"Besieger of the heart, the long adored;
And I shall know him by his regal tread,
And by the grace peculiar to my lord.
Upon my mouth his lips shall be a sword;
Splendid is he by whom this breast shall fall,
This hive of honey burst, this fruit be cored."—
So beauty that would be a willing thrall
Kept vigil, eyes aglow, ear tuned to hear his call.

Had she not had her dream, she might have seen
For what he was the stranger at her gate,
And known his rugged hands, strong mouth, and lean
Hawk-face spelled out for her a star-spun fate.
But captive to a dream she let him wait

In vain for any word she might have said
Whereat he might declare himself her mate.
She looked him through as one unknown or dead;
He passed, an unseen halo blazing round his head.

The grave will be her only lover now,
Though still she watches for the shining one,
Her prince in purple robes, with flaming brow,
Astride a wild steed lineaged from the sun.
Season to season shades, the long days run
To longer years; she still is waiting there,
Not knowing long ago her siege was done,
Not dreaming it has been her bitter share
To entertain her heart's high guest all unaware.

To Lovers of Earth: Fair Warning

Give over to high things the fervent thought
You waste on Earth; let down the righteous bar
Against a wayward peace too dearly bought
Upon this pale and passion-frozen star.
Sweethearts and friends, are they not loyal? Far
More fickle, false, perverse, far more unkind
Is Earth to those who give her heart and mind.

And you whose lusty youth her snares intrigue,
Who glory in her seas, swear by her clouds,
With Age, man's foe, Earth ever is in league.
Time resurrects her even while he crowds

Your bloom to dust, and lengthens out your shrouds
A day's length or a year's; she will be young,
When your last cracked and quivering note is sung.

She will remain the Earth, sufficient still,
Though you are gone and with you that rare loss
That vanishes with your bewildered will.
And there shall flame no red, indignant cross
For you, no quick white scar of wrath emboss
The sky, no blood drip from a wounded moon,
And not a single star chime out of tune.

One of Charles Cullen's decorations for *Copper Sun* (1927)

VARIA

In Spite of Death

All things confirm me in the thought that dust,
Once raised to monumental pride of breath,
To no extent affirms the right of death
To raze such splendor to an ancient crust.
"Grass withereth, the flower fadeth;" yea,
But in the violated seed exults,
The bleakest winter through, a deathless pulse,
Beating, "Spring wipes this sacrilege away."

No less shall I in some new fashion flare
Again, when death has blown my candles out;
Although my blood went down in shameful rout
Tonight, by all this living frame holds fair,
Though death should closet me tonight, I swear
Tomorrow's sun would find his cupboard bare.

Cor Cordium*

Cor cordium is written there,
But the heart of hearts is away;
They could not fashion any bier
To hold that burning clay.

*Written at the Shelley Memorial in Rome, August 1926.

Imprisoned in the flesh, he wrought
Till Death as Prospero,
Pitied the spark that life had caught,
Loosed him, and let him go.

Look, a light like a sun-girt flask;
Listen, and hear it sing.
Light and song are what, you ask?
Ariel off on the wing!

Lines to My Father

The many sow, but only the chosen reap;
Happy the wretched host if Day be brief,
That with the cool oblivion of sleep
A dawnless Night may soothe the smart of grief.

If from the soil our sweat enriches sprout
One meagre blossom for our hands to cull,
Accustomed indigence provokes a shout
Of praise that life becomes so bountiful.

Now ushered regally into your own,
Look where you will, as far as eye can see,
Your little seeds are to a fullness grown,
And golden fruit is ripe on every tree.

Yours is no fairy gift, no heritage
Without travail, to which weak wills aspire;

This is a merited and grief-earned wage
From One Who holds His servants worth their hire.

So has the shyest of your dreams come true,
Built not of sand, but of the solid rock,
Impregnable to all that may accrue
Of elemental rage: storm, stress, and shock.

Protest

(*To John Trounstine*)

I long not now, a little while at least,
For that serene interminable hour
When I shall leave this Barmecidal feast
With poppy for my everlasting flower;
I long not now for that dim cubicle
Of earth to which my lease will not expire,
Where he who comes a tenant there may dwell
Without a thought of famine, flood, or fire.

Surely that house has quiet to bestow—
Still tongue, spent pulse, heart pumped of its last throb,
The fingers tense and tranquil in a row,
The throat unwelled with any sigh or sob—
But time to live, to love, bear pain and smile,
Oh, we are given such a little while!

An Epitaph

(*For Amy Lowell*)

She leans across a golden table,
   Confronts God with an eye
Still puzzled by the standard label
   All flesh bears: Made to die—
And questions Him if He is able
   To reassure her why.

Scandal and Gossip

Scandal is a stately lady,
Whispers when she talks;
Waves of innuendo
Ripple where she walks.

Speaking with a lifted shoulder,
Flicker of a lash,
Scorning words as dangerous,
She is never rash.

Gossip is a giddy girl
Running here and there,
Showing all the neighborhood
What she has to wear.

Gossip babbles like a brook,
Rages like a flood,

Chews her placid hearsays
As a cow her cud.

Scandal hobnobs with the rich
Over purple wine;
Gossip has the vagabonds
In to chat and dine.

Scandal never visits us;
We are far too poor;
Gossip never missed a day
Knocking at our door.

Youth Sings a Song of Rosebuds

(*To Roberta*)

Since men grow diffident at last,
And care no whit at all,
If spring be come, or the fall be past,
Or how the cool rains fall,

I come to no flower but I pluck,
I raise no cup but I sip,
For a mouth is the best of sweets to suck;
The oldest wine's on the lip.

If I grow old in a year or two,
And come to the querulous song
Of "Alack and aday" and "This was true,
And that, when I was young,"

I must have sweets to remember by,
Some blossom saved from the mire,
Some death-rebellious ember I
Can fan into a fire.

Hunger

(*To Emerson Whithorne*)

Break me no bread however white it be;
It cannot fill the emptiness I know;
No wine can cool this desert thirst in me
Though it had lain a thousand years in snow;
No swooning lotus flower's languid juice
Drips anodyne unto my restlessness,
And impotent to win me to a truce
Is every artifice of loveliness.
Inevitable is the way I go,
False-faced amid a pageant permeate
With bliss, yet visioning a higher wave
Than this weak ripple washing to and fro;
The fool still keeps his dreams inviolate
Till their virginity espouse the grave.

Lines to Our Elders

(*To Melanie*)

You too listless to examine
If in pestilence or famine
Death lurk least, a hungry gamin
Gnawing on you like a beaver
On a root, while you trifle
Time away nodding in the sun,
Careless how the shadows crawl
Surely up your crumbling wall,
Heedless of the Thief's footfall,
Death's whose nimble fingers rifle
Your heartbeats one by weary one,—
Here's the difference in our dying:
You go dawdling, we go flying.
Here's a thought flung out to plague you:
Ours the pleasure if we'd liever
Burn completely with the fever
Than go ambling with the ague.

The Poet

Lest any forward thought intrude
Of death and desolation,
Upon a mind shaped but to brood
On wonder and creation,
He keeps an unremittent feud
Against such usurpation.

His ears are tuned to all sharp cries
Of travail and complaining,
His vision stalks a new moon's rise
In every old moon's waning,
And in his heart pride's red flag flies
Too high for sorrow's gaining.

Thus militant, with sword in hand,
His battle shout renewing,
He feels all faith affords is planned,
As seeds, for rich accruing;
Death ties no knot too gordianed
For his deft hands' undoing.

More Than a Fool's Song

(*To Edward Perry*)

Go look for beauty where you least
Expect to hear her hive;
Regale your belly with a feast
Of hunger till you thrive.

For honest treatment seek the thief;
For truth consult the liar;
Court pleasure in the halls of grief;
Find smoothness on a briar.

The worth impearled in chastity
Is known best of the harlot,

And courage throws her panoply
On many a native varlet.

In Christian practice those who move
To symbols strange to us
May reckon clearer of His love
Than we who own His cross.

The world's a curious riddle thrown
Water-wise from heaven's cup;
The souls we think are hurtling down
Perhaps are climbing up.

And When I Think

(*For one just dead*)

And when I think how that dark throat of thine,
Irreconcilably stilled, lies mute,
A golden honey-hive robbed of its fruit,
A wassail cup in which there is no wine;
Thy sweet, high treble hushed that never mine
Auricular delight again shall suit
To wild bird warblings, or liken to a flute
That with wild tremors agitates the spine;
Then though the legion-throated spring cry out,
Though raucously the summer whirl about
Me all her scent and color in one shout
Of pride, though autumn clamor at my ear,
Or winter crackle round me, crystal-clear,
While memory persists, I do not hear.

Advice to a Beauty

(To Sydonia)

Of all things, lady, be not proud;
Inter not beauty in that shroud
Wherein the living waste, the dead,
Unwept and unrememberéd,
Decay. Beauty beats so frail a wing;
Suffer men to gaze, poets to sing
How radiant you are, compare
And favor you to that most rare
Bird of delight: a lovely face
Matched with an equal inner grace.
Sweet bird, beware the Fowler, Pride;
His knots once neatly crossed and tied,
The prey is caged and walled about
With no way in and no way out.

Ultimatum

I hold not with the fatalist creed
Of what must be must be;
There is enough to meet my need
In this most meagre me.

These two slim arms were made to rein
My steed, to ward and fend;
There is more gold in this small brain
Than I can ever spend.

The seed I plant is chosen well;
Ambushed by no sly sweven,
I plant it if it droops to hell,
Or if it blooms to heaven.

Lines Written in Jerusalem*

A city builded on a hill may flaunt
Its glory in the sunken valley's face,
And ways the Nazarene has trod may vaunt
A credible inheritance of grace.
Your very stones, Jerusalem, can sing:
"He would have taken us beneath His wing."

*August 1926

On the Mediterranean Sea*

That weaver of words, the poet who
First named this sullen sea the blue,
And left off painting there, he knew
How rash a man would be to try
Precise defining of such a dye
As lurks within this colored spume.
And for retelling little room
He willed to singers then unborn
But destined later years, at morn,
High noon, twilight, or night to view

This Protean sheet, and anguish through
The mind to paint its wayward hue.
Not Helen's eyes, no vaunted stains
That shone in Cressid's lacy veins,
Not those proud fans the peacocks spread,
No sky that ever arched its head
Above a wonder-stricken two
Aghast at love, wore such a hue.
Only the Hand that never erred
Bent on beauty, creation-spurred,
Could mix and mingle such a dye,
Nor leave its like in earth or sky.
That sire of singers, the poet who
First named this sullen sea the blue
And left off painting there, he knew!

*July 15, 1926

Millennial

(*To John Haynes Holmes*)

Once in a thousand years a call may ring
Divested so of every cumbering lie,
A man espousing it may fight and sing,
And count it but a little thing to die;
Once in a thousand years a star may come,
Six-pointed, tipped with such an astral flow,
Its singing sisters must bow hushed in dumb,
Half-mutinous, yet half-adoring show.

Once in as many years a man may rise
So cosmopolitan of thought and speech,
Humanity reflected in his eyes,
His heart a haven every race can reach,
That doubters shall receive a mortal thrust,
And own, "This man proves flesh exalts its dust."

At the Wailing Wall in Jerusalem

Of all the grandeur that was Solomon's
High testament of Israel's far pride,
Shedding its lustre like a sun of suns,
This feeble flicker only has not died.
This wall alone reminds a vanquished race,
This brief remembrance still retained in stone,
That sure foundations guard their given place
To rehabilitate the overthrown.

So in the battered temple of the heart,
That grief is harder on than time on stone,
Though three sides crumble, one will stand apart,
Where thought may mourn its past, remembrance
    groan,
And hands now bare that once were rich with rings
Rebuild upon the ancient site of things.

To Endymion*

Endymion, your star is steadfast now,
Beyond aspersion's power to glitter down;
There is no redder blossom on the bough
Of song, no richer jewel in her crown;
Long shall she stammer forth a broken note,
(Striving with how improvident a tongue)
Before the ardor of another throat
Transcends the jubilate you have sung.

High as the star of that last poignant cry
Death could not stifle in the wasted frame,
You know at length the bright immortal lie
Time gives to those detractors of your name,
And see, from where you and Diana ride,
Your humble epitaph—how misapplied!

*Rome, August 1926, after a visit to the grave of Keats.

Epilogue

The lily, being white not red,
    Contemns the vivid flower,
And men alive believe the dead
    Have lost their vital power.

Yet some prefer the brilliant shade,
    And pass the livid by;
And no man knows if dead men fade
    Or bloom, save those that die.

JUVENILIA

Open Door

Once I held my heart's door full wide
That love might enter in;
I saw him pass in peacock pride,
Nor cast a glance within.

The door stands wide by night and day,
The lamp burns on though dim,
Lest some lone traveler lose his way.
(Love thinks it burns for him.)

Disenchantment

This is the circle fairies drew
To hold your love and mine,
And here it was the tall tree grew
With fruit we bruised for wine.

Serene we stand where once we stood
Scarce breathing, tense, alert;
Now nothing stirs for ill or good,
For healing or for hurt.

Your hands are cold, and I am cold;
We speak, but drop no pearls;
No careless wind disturbs the gold
Still cradled in your curls.

Call—yet no agile echo leaps
A mountain for our grief;
No slant-eyed fawn for terror creeps
Along a trembling leaf.

If once I had a fairy club,
You had a wonder stone,
And did I wave or you but rub,
The world was all our own.

This is the circle; see, I wave
My wand, you rub your stone;
But nothing's here except a grave
On which cold winds have blown.

Leaves

One, two, and three,
Dead leaves drift from a tree.

Yesterday they loved
Wind and rain, the brush
Of wings
Soft and clean, that moved
Through them beyond the crush
Of things.
Yesterday they loved.

Yesterday they sang
Silver symphonies,
Raised high
Holy chants that rang
Leaf-wise through their trees;
As I,
Yesterday they sang.

Unremembered now,
They will soon lie warm
With snow;
They could grace a bough
Once, and love and charm,
Although
Unremembered now.

Trees so soon forget
Little leaves they had
Before,
Knowing spring will let
Them wake, vernal clad
With more;
Trees so soon forget.

Man dreams that he
Is more than a leaf on a tree.

Song

Love, unto me be song of bird;
So soon the song is through;
I would I had a brazen word
To brand this truth untrue.

Love, unto me be life's full sun,
Unmindful of your light;
So soon the stealthy shadows run
All days into one night.

There is a word that must be spoken,
A word your heart would hear,
And mine must whisper, or be broken;
Oh, make your heart your ear.

The Touch

I am no longer lame since Spring
Stooped to me where I lay,
And charmed with flute and silver lute
My laggard limbs to play.
Her voice is sweet as long-stored wine;
I leap like a hounded fawn;
I rise and follow over hill and hollow
To the flush of the crimson dawn!

A Poem Once Significant, Now Happily Not

Whatever I have loved has wounded me;
I bear unto my grave this crimson scar,
The vivid testament of how a star
Can hurt; and I am blinded by the sea.
Hell-deep and heaven-high for Beauty's sake,
Pierced with the shaft that rankles ere it kills,
I danced with dawn and dusk upon their hills,
Yet thought at each earth kiss my heart would break.

Small wonder is it, love, that you who are
Far lovelier than sea, dawn-flush, or star,
Or spittled clay grown arrogant with breath,
Beholding this maimed thing that dares to crawl
To your imperial bosom, should let fall
Your hand, betrothing Insolence to Death.

Under the Mistletoe

I did not know she'd take it so,
Or else I'd never dared;
Although the bliss was worth the blow,
I did not know she'd take it so.
She stood beneath the mistletoe
So long I thought she cared;
I did not know she'd take it so,
Or else I'd never dared.

THE BALLAD OF THE BROWN GIRL: AN OLD BALLAD RETOLD | 1927

Oh, this is the tale the grandams tell
In the land where the grass is blue,
And some there are who say 'tis false,
And some that hold it true.

      * * *

Lord Thomas on a summer's day
Came to his mother's door;
His eyes were ringed for want of sleep;
His heart was troubled sore.

He knelt him at his mother's side;
She stroked his curly head.
"I've come to be advised of you;
Advise me well," he said.

"For there are two who love me well—
I wot it from each mouth—
And one's Fair London, lily maid,
And pride of all the south.

She is full shy and sweet as still
Delight when nothing stirs;
My soul can thrive on love of her,
And all my heart is hers."

His mother's slender fingers ploughed
Dark furrows through his hair,
"The other one who loves you well,
Is she as sweet and fair?"

"She is the dark Brown Girl who knows
No more-defining name,
And bitter tongues have worn their tips
In sneering at her shame."

"But there are lands to go with her,
And gold and silver stores."
His mother whispered in his ear,
"And all her heart is yours."

His mother loved the clink of gold,
The odor and the shine
Of larders bowed with venison
And crystal globes of wine.

"Oh, love is good," the lady quoth,
"When berries ripe and sweet,
From every bush and weighted vine
Are crying, 'Take and eat'."

"But what is best when winter comes
Is gold and silver bright;
Go bring me home the nut-brown maid
And leave the lily-white."

He sent his criers through the land
To cry his wedding day,
But bade them at Fair London's road
To turn the other way.

His bridal day dawned white and fair,
His heart held night within;
He heard its anguished beats above
The jocund wedding din.

The Brown Girl came to him as might
A queen to take her crown;
With gems her fingers flamed and flared;
Her robe was weighted down.

Her hair was black as sin is black
And ringed about with fire;
Her eyes were black as night is black
When moon and stars conspire;
Her mouth was one red cherry clipt
In twain, her voice a lyre.

Lord Thomas took her jewelled hand,
The holy words were said,
And they have made the holy vow
To share one board and bed.

But suddenly the furious feast
Is shattered with a shout;
Lord Thomas trembles at the word,
"Fair London is without."

All pale and proud she stands without,
And will not venture in;
He leaves the side of his nut-brown bride
To bid her enter in.

Her skin was white as almond milk
Slow trickling from the flower;
Her frost-blue eyes were darkening
Like clouds before a shower;

Her thin pink lips were twin rosebuds
That had not come to flower,
And crowning all, her golden hair
Was loosened out in shower.

He has taken her by her slim white hand,
(Oh, light was her hand in his)
But the touch ran wild and fierce and hot,
And burned like a brand in his.

"Lord Thomas," she said; her voice was low,
"I come unbidden here,
But I have come to see your bride
And taste your bridal cheer."

He has taken her by her slim white hand
And led her to his bride,
And brown and white have bent them low,
And sat them side by side.

He has brimmed a cup with the wedding wine,
He has placed it in her hand,
She has raised it high and smiled on him
Like love in a distant land.

"I came to see your bonny bride,
I came to wish you well,"
Her voice was clear as song is clear;
Clear as a silver bell.

"But, Thomas, Lord, is this your bride?
I think she's mighty brown;
Why didn't you marry a fair, bright girl
As ever the sun shone on?

For only the rose and the rose should mate,
Oh, never the hare and the hound,"
And the wine he poured for her crimson mouth
She poured upon the ground.

The flow of wine and jest has ceased,
The groom has flushed and paled,
The Brown Girl's lips are moist and red
Where her sharp white teeth assailed.

Dark wrath has climbed her nut-brown throat,
And wrath in her wild blood sings,
But she tramples her passions underfoot
Because she comes of kings.

She has taken her stand by her rival's side,
"Lord Thomas, you have heard,
As I am yours and you are mine
By ring and plighted word,
Avenge me here on our bridal day."—
Lord Thomas spoke no word.

The Brown Girl's locks were held in place
By a dagger serpentine;
Thin it was and long and sharp,
And tempered well and fine.

And legend claimed that a dusky queen,
In a dusky dream-lit land,
Had loved in vain, and died of it,
By her own slim twilight hand.

The Brown Girl's hair has kissed her waist,
Her hand has closed on steel;
Fair London's blood has joined the wine
She sullied with her heel.

Lord Thomas caught her as she fell,
And cried, "My sweet, my fair,
Dark night has hid the golden sun,
And blood has thicked the air.

The little hand that should have worn
A golden band for me,
The little hand that fluttered so
Is still as death can be."

He bent and kissed the weeping wound
Fresh in her heart's young core,
And then he kissed her sleeping mouth
That would not waken more.

He seized the Brown Girl's rippling hair
That swung in eddies loose,
And with one circle of his arm
He made a hairy noose.

He pulled it till she swooned for pain,
And spat a crimson lake;
He pulled it till a something snapped
That was not made to break.

And her he loved he brought and placed
By her who was his bride,
And brown and white like broken buds
Kept vigil side by side.

And one was like a white, white rose
Whose inmost heart has bled,
And one was like a red, red rose
Whose roots have witherèd.

Lord Thomas took a golden harp
That hung above his head;
He picked its strings and played a tune
And sang it to the dead.

"He picked its strings and played a tune
And sang it to the dead."
Centerfold illustration from the first edition of
The Ballad of the Brown Girl (1927), by Charles Cullen

"O lovers never barter love
For gold or fertile lands,
For love is meat and love is drink,
And love heeds love's commands."

"And love is shelter from the rain,
And scowling stormy skies;
Who casts off love must break his heart,
And rue it till he dies."

And then he hugged himself and grinned,
And laughed, "Ha, ha," for glee;
But those who watched knew he was mad,
And shudderèd to see.

And some made shift to go to him,
But there was in his eye
What made each man to turn aside
To let his neighbor by.

His mother in a satin gown
Was fain to go to him,
But his lips curled back like a gray wolf's fang,
When the huntsmen blow to him.

"No mother of mine, for gold's the god
Before whose feet you fall;
Here be two dead who will be three,
And you have slain us all.

Go dig one grave to hold us all
And make it deep and wide;
And lay the Brown Girl at my feet,
Fair London by my side."

And as he spoke his hand went up,
And singing steel swept down,
And as its kiss betrayed his heart,
Death wore a triple crown.

And in the land where the grass is blue,
In a grave dug deep and wide,
The Brown Girl sleeps at her true lord's feet,
Fair London by his side.

Frontispiece to *The Black Christ & Other Poems* (1929)

VARIA

To the Three for Whom the Book

Once like a lady
In a silken dress,
The serpent might eddy
Through the wilderness,
Billow and glow
And undulate
In a rustling flow
Of sinuous hate.
Now dull-eyed and leaden,
Of having lost
His Eden
He pays the cost.
He shuns the tree
That brought him low
As grown to be
Domestic; no
Temptations dapple,
From leaf to root,
The modern apple
Our meekest fruit.
Dragon and griffin

And basilisk
Whose stare could stiffen,
And the hot breath whisk
From the overbold
Braving a gaze
So freezing cold,
Who sings their praise
These latter days?
That venomous head
On a woman fair,—
Medusa's dead
Of the hissing hair.
No beasts are made
Meet for the whir
Of that sunken blade
Excalibur.
No smithies forge
A shining sword
Fit for the gorge
Of a beast abhorred.
Pale Theseus
Would have no need,
Were he with us,
Of sword or thread;
For long has been set
The baleful star
Of Pasiphaë's pet,
The Minotaur.
Though they are dead,
Those ancient ones,
Each bestial head

Dust under tons
Of dust, new beasts
Have come, their heirs,
Claiming their feasts
As the old did theirs.
Clawless they claw,
Fangless they rend;
And the stony maw
Crams on without end.
Still are arrayed
(But with brighter eyes)
Stripling and maid
For the sacrifice.
We cannot spare
This toll we pay
Of the slender, the fair,
The bright and the gay!
Gold and black crown,
Body slim and taut,
How they go down
'Neath the juggernaut!
Youth of the world,
Like scythèd wheat,
How they are hurled
At the clay god's feet!
Hear them cry Holy
To stone and to steel,
See them bend lowly,
Loyal and leal,
Blood rendered and bone,
To steel and to stone.

They have forgot
The stars and the sun,
The grassy plot,
And waters that run
From rock to rock;—
Their only care
Is to grasp a lock
Of Mammon's hair.

But you three rare
Friends whom I love
(With rhymes to swear
The depths whereof)
A book to you three
Who have not bent
The idolatrous knee,
Nor worship lent
To modern rites,
Knowing full well
How a just god smites
The infidel;
Three to whom Pan
Is no mere myth,
But a singing Man
To be reckoned with;—
Witness him now
In the mist and dew;
Lean and hear how
He carols to you:
"Gather as a flower
Living to your heart;
Let the full shower

Rankle and smart;
Youth is the coffer
Where all is hid;
All age may offer
Youth can outbid.
Blind with your beauty
The ranks of scorn,
Take for a duty
Pleasure; you were born
Joy to incur.
Ere the eyes are misted
With a rheumy blur,
Ere the speech is twisted
To a throaty slur,
Ere the cheeks are haggard;
Ere the prick of the spur
Finds you lame or laggard,
Do not demur!
When Time advances
Terrible and lone,
Recall there were dances
Though they be flown.
When Death plys the riddle
To which all are mute,
Remember the fiddle,
The lyre and the flute."

To three who will heed
His song, nor brook
That a god should plead
In vain, a book.

Tribute

(*To My Mother*)

Because man is not virtuous in himself,
Nor kind, nor given to sweet charities,
Save goaded by the little kindling elf
Of some dear face it pleasures him to please;
Some men who else were humbled to the dust,
Have marveled that the chastening hand should stay,
And never dreamed they held their lives in trust
To one the victor loved a world away.
So I, least noble of a churlish race,
Least kind of those by nature rough and crude,
Have at the intervention of your face
Spared him with whom was my most bitter feud
One moment, and the next, a deed more grand,
The helpless fly imprisoned in my hand.

That Bright Chimeric Beast

(*For Lynn Riggs*)

That bright chimeric beast
Conceived yet never born,
Save in the poet's breast,
The white-flanked unicorn,
Never may be shaken
From his solitude;
Never may be taken
In any earthly wood.

That bird forever feathered,
Of its new self the sire,
After aeons weathered,
Reincarnate by fire,
Falcon may not nor eagle
Swerve from his aerie,
Nor any crumb inveigle
Down to an earthly tree.

That fish of the dread regime
Invented to become
The fable and the dream
Of the Lord's aquarium,
Leviathan, the jointed
Harpoon was never wrought
By which the Lord's anointed
Will suffer to be caught.

Bird of the deathless breast,
Fish of the frantic fin,
That bright chimeric beast
Flashing the argent skin,—
If beasts like these you'd harry,
Plumb then the poet's dream;
Make it your aviary,
Make it your wood and stream.
There only shall the swish
Be heard, of the regal fish;
There like a golden knife
Dart the feet of the unicorn,
And there, death brought to life,
The dead bird be reborn.

At the Étoile

(At the Unknown Soldier's Grave in Paris)

If in the lists of life he bore him well,
Sat gracefully or fell unhorsed in love,
No tongue is dowered now with speech to tell
Since he and death somewhere matched glove with
    glove.

What proud or humble union gave him birth,
Not reckoning on this immortal bed,
Is one more riddle that the cryptic earth
Though knowing chooses to retain unsaid.

Since he was weak as other men,—or like
Young Galahad as fair in thought as limb,
Each bit of moving dust in France may strike
Its breast in pride, knowing he stands for him.

Two Epitaphs

I   FOR THE UNKNOWN SOLDIER (PARIS)

Unknown but not unhonored rest,
Symbol of all Time shall not reap;
Not one stilled heart in that torn breast,
But a myriad millions sleep.

Here sleeps a spark that never burned,
A seed not granted spring to bloom,
A soul whose darkened pathway turned
From tomb of flesh to dusty tomb.

To an Unknown Poet

"Love is enough," I read somewhere;
Lines some poor poet in his pride
And poverty wrote on the air
To ease his heart, and soothe his bride.

Something in me, child of an age
Cold to the core, undeified,
Warmed to my brother bard, this sage;
And I too leaned upon my pride.

But pride I found can blind our eyes,
And poverty is worse than pride.
Love's breed from both is a nest of lies;
And singer of sweet songs, you lied.

Little Sonnet to Little Friends

Let not the proud of heart condemn
Me that I mould my ways to hers,
Groping for healing in a hem

No wind of passion ever stirs;
Nor let them sweetly pity me
When I am out of sound and sight;
They waste their time and energy;
No mares encumber me at night.

Always a trifle fond and strange,
And some have said a bit bizarre,
Say, "Here's the sun," I would not change
It for my dead and burnt-out star.
Shine as it will, I have no doubt
Some day the sun, too, may go out.

Mood

I think an impulse stronger than my mind
May some day grasp a knife, unloose a vial,
Or with a little leaden ball unbind
The cords that tie me to the rank and file.
My hands grow quarrelsome with bitterness,
And darkly bent upon the final fray;
Night with its stars upon a grave seems less
Indecent than the too complacent day.

God knows I would be kind, let live, speak fair,
Requite an honest debt with more than just,
And love for Christ's dear sake these shapes that wear
A pride that had its genesis in dust,—
The meek are promised much in a book I know
But one grows weary turning cheek to blow.

Counter Mood

Let this be scattered far and wide, laid low
Upon the waters as they fall and rise,
Be caught and carried by the winds that blow,
Nor let it be arrested by the skies:
I who am mortal say I shall not die;
I who am dust of this am positive,
That though my nights tend toward the grave, yet I
Shall on some brighter day arise, and live.

Ask me not how I am oracular,
Nor whence this arrogant assurance springs.
Ask rather Faith the canny conjurer,
(Who while your reason mocks him mystifies
Winning the grudging plaudits of your eyes)—
How suddenly the supine egg has wings.

The Wind and the Weather

Forever shall not burn his tongue
    So glibly after this;
Eternity was brief that hung
    Upon a passing kiss.

A year ago no metaphor
    Was rich enough to trace
A single figure boasting more
    Allurement than her face.

One spring from then, small change we find
    In him; she still is fair.
But in the other's heart or mind
    Neither glows anywhere.

In the Midst of Life

Bud bursting from a tomb
Of dust, this mortal knows
In winter's sterile womb
For your despoiling grows
What comes to every rose.

Grass so securely green,
Sky-climbing corn so tall,
Know in your length is seen
What overtowers all:
The shadow of the fall.

Yet blossoms with each spring
Reopen; grasses sprout;
And jaunty corn stalks fling
New skeins of silk about.
Nature is skilled to rout

Death's every ambuscade;
For man alone is poured
The potion once essayed
That sharper than a sword
Destroys both mouth and gourd.

Deplore, lament, bewail;
The sword seeks out the sheath;
Though all things else may fail,
Two things keep faith; this breath
A while; and longer death.

Minutely Hurt

Since I was minutely hurt,
Giant griefs and woes
Only find me staunchly girt
Against all other blows.

Once an atom cracks the heart
All is done and said;
Poison, steel, and fiery dart
May then be buffeted.

Never the Final Stone

Though by the glory of your lady's face
The riots of the sun and moon are quelled,
Yet have the hands that fashioned her some grace
Whereto perfection was allied, withheld.

The perfect wooer never speaks the word
The object of his passion most would hear;
So does expectance keep her wild feet spurred
Toward that which ever is no more than near.

And daily from His lonely mountain-top,
God sees us rear our Babels on the plain;
Then with one stone to go, He lets us drop
That we may want and strive for Him again.

Light Lady

They say when virtue slipped from her,
Awakened by her fall,
Sin seemed to work a miracle
And made her soul grow tall.

Here with her penny papers by,
We see how well she diced:
Nothing to do but munch her gums
And sing the love of Christ.

And now with alms for what she was
Men stroke her ragged fur;
When Death comes down this street, his face
Will not be strange to her.

By Their Fruits

I know a lover when I see one,
And I can tell the way they fare:
If those they dote on shed some sun,
Or blow a cool and languid air.

Those that are loved, though niggardly,
Move with a lively foot and eye;
The others drag like men who see
Their day and minute set to die.

A Miracle Demanded

This life is like a tree that flourisheth
With fruit and flower, gay leaf and sprouting twig;
But pestilence is in the wind's warm breath,
And at the roots the worms and mice grow big.
The gardener, steady in his anxious claims,
Who prunes for love, he says, and not for wage,
Than simple care has more disastrous names,
The most elect: Disease, Death, and Old Age.

Against such foes how shall a tree prevail
To curb its consummation in decay,
And like a tree shall men not strive and fail,
Unless all wonders have not passed away?
Renew an ancient vision, Lord, in me:
Open the young man's eyes that he may see.

Tongue-tied

You ask me why I love her, and you pause
Magnanimous, that I may make reply
Handing you deftly parceled every cause,

Saying with confidence, "Lo, this is why."
But I am mute as if I had no tongue,
Without reason as if I had no mind,
This song the most familiar ever sung,
Is lost to me like a leaf caught in the wind.

And so my tongue is tied; and so you smile
Not knowing, little lover that you are,
(Prattling, "'Twill wear, 'twill last so long a while")
The poet is compelled to love his star,
Not knowing he could never tell you why
Though silence makes inadequate reply.

Ultima Verba

Not being in my coffin, yet I know
What suffocations crowd their breath who go
Through some mischance alive into the grave;
Not having any wound at all to shout
Belief to Thomas who must see or doubt,
I feel my life blood ebbing wave on wave.

And yet this knowledge cannot summon strength
To rend apart the life-impaling length
Of these strong boards that hold my body down;
There is no cloth, no cool and radiant stuff
(Save fashioned by your hand) healing enough
To staunch this thin red flow in which I drown.

I am as one knowing what day he dies,
Who looks in vain for mercy into eyes
No glints of pity shade, no pardons stir,
And thinks, "Although the trap by which I span
This world and that another springs, this man
Is both my judge and executioner."

The Foolish Heart

"Be still, heart, cease those measured strokes;
Lie quiet in your hollow bed;
This moving frame is but a hoax
To make you think you are not dead."

Thus spake I to my body's slave,
With beats still to be answerèd;
Poor foolish heart that needs a grave
To prove to it that it is dead.

A Wish

I hope when I have sung my rounds
Of song, I shall have strength to slay
The wish to chirp on any grounds,
Content that silence hold her sway,
My tongue not rolling futile sounds
After my heart has had its say.

For Helen Keller

Against our puny sound and sight
In vain the bells of Heaven ring,
The Mystic Blossoms red and white
May not intrigue our visioning.

For lest we handle, lest we touch,
Lest carnally our minds condone,
Our clumsy credence may not clutch
The under or the overtone.

Her finer alchemy converts
The clanging brass to golden-pealed,
And for her sight the black earth spurts
Hues never thought there unrevealed.

Asked and Answered

How have I found this favor in your sight,
And will the flame burn steady to the end,
Until we pass that dark and dangerous bend
Where there is such a crying need for light;
Or will it flare up now, flame-clear and bright,
Sun-like its wealth so far and wide distend
That nothing will remain for us to spend
When toll is taken of the dismal night?

Why should I harrow up my mind like this
To tarnish with a doubt each golden kiss?
This is the Day most certainly. This bars
Us now from any hidden darkness spun.
Sufficient to the day let be the sun,
And to the night the spear-points of the stars.

Two Poets

1

"The love-mad lark you sing of swooned," they said,
"And speared his bosom on a thorn of last
Year's rose; cease playing Orpheus; no blast
You blow can raise Eurydice once dead.
Our ears are cloyed with songs our fathers heard
Of how your lady's face and form were fair;
Put by your fluting; swell a martial air,
And spur us on with some prophetic word."

So, wearying, he changed his tune, and won
The praise of little men (who needed none) . . .
But oh to see him smile as when dawn blew
A trumpet only he could hear, and dew
He could not brush away besieged his eyes
At sight of gulls departing from his skies.

2

"How could a woman love him; love, or wed?"
And thinking only of his tuneless face
And arms that held no hint of skill or grace,

They shook a slow, commiserative head
To see him amble by; but still they fed
Their wilting hearts on his, were fired to race
Once more, and panting at life's deadly pace,
They drank as wine the blood-in-song he shed.

Yet in the dream-walled room where last he lay,
Soft garments gathered dust all night and day,
As women whom he loved and sang of came
To smooth his brow and wail a secret name.
A rose placed in his hand by Guinevere
Was drenched with Magdalen's eternal tear.

Not Sacco and Vanzetti

These men who do not die, but send to death,
These iron men whom mercy cannot bend
Beyond the lettered law; what when their breath
Shall suddenly and naturally end?
What shall their final retribution be,
What bloody silver then shall pay the tolls
Exacted for this legal infamy
When death indicts their stark immortal souls?

The day a slumbering but awful God,
Before Time to Eternity is blown,
Examines with the same unyielding rod
These images of His with hearts of stone,
These men who do not die, but death decree,—
These are the men I should not care to be.

A Song No Gentleman
Would Sing to Any Lady

There were some things I might not know
Had you not pedagogued me so;
And these I thank you for;
Now never shall a piquant face
Cause my tutored heart a trace
Of anguish any more.

Before your pleasure made me wise
A simulacrum of disguise
Masked the serpent and the dove;
That I discern now hiss from coo,
My heart's full gratitude to you,
Lady I had learned to love.

Before I knew love well I sang
Many a polished pain and pang
With proper bardic zeal;
But now I know hearts do not break
So easily, and though a snake
Has made them, wounds may heal.

Self Criticism

Shall I go all my bright days singing,
(A little pallid, a trifle wan)
The failing note still vainly clinging
To the throat of the stricken swan?

Shall I never feel and meet the urge
To bugle out beyond my sense
That the fittest song of earth is a dirge,
And only fools trust Providence?

Than this better the reed never turned flute,
Better than this no song,
Better a stony silence, better a mute
Mouth and a cloven tongue.

A Thorn Forever in the Breast

A hungry cancer will not let him rest
Whose heart is loyal to the least of dreams;
There is a thorn forever in his breast
Who cannot take his world for what it seems;
Aloof and lonely must he ever walk,
Plying a strange and unaccustomed tongue,
An alien to the daily round of talk,
Mute when the sordid songs of earth are sung.

This is the certain end his dream achieves:
He sweats his blood and prayers while others sleep,
And shoulders his own coffin up a steep
Immortal mountain, there to meet his doom
Between two wretched dying men, of whom
One doubts, and one for pity's sake believes.

The Proud Heart

That lively organ, palpitant and red,
Enrubied in the staid and sober breast,
Telling the living man, "You are not dead
Until this hammered anvil takes its rest,"
My life's timepiece wound to alarm some day
The body to its need of box and shroud,
Was meant till then to beat one haughty way;
A crimson stroke should be no less than proud.

Yet this high citadel has come to grief,
Been broken as an arrow drops its bird,
Splintered as many ways as veins in a leaf
At a woman's laugh or a man's harsh word;
But being proud still strikes its hours in pain;
The dead man lives, and none perceives him slain.

INTERLUDE

The Simple Truth

I know of all the words I speak or write,
Precious and woven of a vibrant sound,
None ever snares your faith, intrigues you quite,
Or sends you soaring from the solid ground.
You are the level-headed lover who
Can match my fever while the kisses last,
But you are never shaken through and through;
Your roots are firm after the storm has passed.

I shall know nights of tossing in my sleep
Fondling a hollow where a head should lie;
But you a calm review, no tears to weep,
No wounds to dress, no futile breaths to sigh.
Ever this was the way of wind with flame:
To harry it, then leave swift as it came.

Therefore, Adieu

Now you are gone, and with your unreturning goes
All I had thought in spite of you would stay;
Now draws forever to its unawakening close
The beauty of the bright bandanna'd day.

Now sift in ombrous flakes and revolutions slow
My dreams descending from my heady sky.
The balm I kept to cool my grief in (leaves of snow)
Now melts, with your departure flowing by.

I knew, indeed, the straight unswerving track the sun
Took to your face (as other ecstasies)
Yet I had thought some faith to me in them; they run
From me to you as fly to honey, bees.

Avid, to leave me neither fevered joy nor ache,
Only of soul and body vast unrest.
Sun, moon, and stars should be enough; why must you
    take
The feeling of the heart out of the breast?

Now I who dreamed before I died to shoot one shaft
Of courage from a warped and crooked bow,
Stand utterly forsaken, stripped of that small craft
I had, watching with you all prowess go.

At a Parting

Let us not turn for this aside to die,
Crying a lover may not be a friend.
Our grief is vast enough without that lie;
All stories may not boast a happy end.
Love was a flower, sweet, and flowers fade;
Love was a fairy tale; these have their close.
The endless chronicle was never made,
Nor, save in dreams, the ever-scented rose.

Seeing them dim in passion's diadem,
Our rubies that were bright that now are dull,
Let them not fade without their requiem,
How they were red one time and beautiful,
And how the heart where once a ruby bled
May live, yet bear that mark till it is dead.

Dictum

Yea, I have put thee from me utterly,
And they who plead thy cause do plead in vain;
Window and door are bolted, never key
From any ore shall cozen them again.
This is my regal justice: banishment,
That those who please me now may read and see
How self-sustained I am, with what content
I thrive alike on love or treachery.

God, Thou hast Christ, they say, at Thy right hand;
Close by Thy left Michael is straight and leal;
Around Thy throne the chanting elders stand,
And on the earth Thy feudal millions kneel.
Criest Thou never, Lord, above their song:
"But Lucifer was tall, his wings were long"?

Revelation

Pity me, I said;
But you cried, Pity you;
And suddenly I saw
Higher than my own grief grew.
I saw a tree of woe so tall,
So deeply boughed with grief,
That matched with it my bitter plant
Was dwarfed into a leaf.

Bright Bindings

Your love to me was like an unread book,
Bright-backed, with smooth white pages yet unslit;
Fondly as a lover, foolishly, I took
It from its shelf one day and opened it.
Here shall I read, I thought, beauty and grace,
The soul's most high and awful poetry:—
Alas for lovers and the faith they place
In love, alas for you, alas for me.

I have but read a page or two at most,
The most my horror-blinded eyes may read.
I find here but a windy tapering ghost
Where I sought flesh gifted to ache and bleed.
Yet back you go, though counterfeit you be.
I love bright books even when they fail me.

Ghosts

Breast under breast when you shall lie
    With him who in my place
Bends over you with flashing eye
    And ever nearing face;

Hand fast in hand when you shall tread
    With him the springing ways
Of love from me inherited
    After my little phase;

Be not surprised if suddenly
    The couch or air confound
Your ravished ears upbraidingly,
    And silence turn to sound.

But never let it trouble you,
    Or cost you one caress;
Ghosts are soon sent with a word or two
    Back to their loneliness.

Song in Spite of Myself

Never love with all your heart,
    It only ends in aching;
And bit by bit to the smallest part
    That organ will be breaking.

Never love with all your mind,
   It only ends in fretting;
In musing on sweet joys behind,
   Too poignant for forgetting.

Never love with all your soul,
   For such there is no ending,
Though a mind that frets may find control,
   And a shattered heart find mending.

Give but a grain of the heart's rich seed,
   Confine some under cover,
And when love goes, bid him God-speed.
   And find another lover.

Nothing Endures

Nothing endures,
Not even love,
Though the warm heart purrs
Of the length thereof.

Though beauty wax,
Yet shall it wane;
Time lays a tax
On the subtlest brain.

Let the blood riot,
Give it its will;
It shall grow quiet,
It shall grow still.

Nirvana gapes
For all things given;
Nothing escapes,
Love not even.

There Must Be Words

This wound will be effaced as others have,
This scar recede into oblivion,
Leaving the skin immaculate and suave,
With none to guess the thing they gaze upon.
After a decent show of mourning I,
As once I ever was, shall be as free
To look on love with calm unfaltering eye,
And marvel that such fools as lovers be.

These are brave words from one who like a child
Cuts dazzling arabesques on summer ice
That, kissed by sun, begins to crack and thaw;
The old assurance dies, only the wild
Desire to live goes on; any device
Compels its frantic grasp, even a straw.

One Day I Told My Love

One day I told my love my heart,
  Disclosed it out and in;

I let her read the ill-writ chart
  Small with virtue, big with sin.

I took it from the hidden socket
  Where it was wont to grieve;
"I'll turn it," I said, "into a locket,
  Or a bright band for your sleeve."

I let her hold the naked thing
  No one had seen before;
And had she willed, her hand might wring
  It dry and drop it to the floor.

It was a gentle thing she did,
  The wisest and the best;
"The proper place for a heart," she said,
  "Is back in the sheltering breast."

Lesson

I lay in silence at her side,
  My heart's and spirit's choice;
For we had said harsh things and cried
  On love in a bitter voice.

We lay and watched two points in space,
  Pricked in heaven, faint and far.
They seemed so near, but who could trace
  That width between star and star?

We lay and watched, and suddenly
    There was a streak of light,
And where were two, the eye might see
    But one star in the night.

My hand stole out, her hand crept near,
    Grief was a splintered spar;
Two fused in one there, did you hear
    Us claiming kinship, star?

The Street Called Crooked

(*Le Havre, August 1928*)

"*Bon soir, monsieur,*" they called to me;
    And, "*Venez voir nos femmes.*"
"*Bon soir, mesdames,*" they got from me,
    And, "*J'ai une meilleure dame.*"

"To meet strange lips and foreign eyes
    I did not cross the foam,
I have a dearer, fairer prize
    Who waits for me at home."

"Her eyes are browner, lips more red
    Than any lady's light;
'Twould grieve her heart and droop her head
    If I failed her tonight."

"Bon soir, mesdames; que Dieu vous garde;
    And catch this coin I throw;
The ways of life are bleak and hard,
    Ladies, I think you know."

A bright and crooked street it gleamed
    With light and laughter filled;
All night the warm wine frothed and streamed
    While souls were stripped and killed.

The Law That Changeth Not

Stern legislation of a Persian hand
Upon my heart, Love, strict Medean writ,
Must till the end of time and me command
Obeisance from him who fostered it.
All other codes may hide their littlest flaw
Toward which the hopeful prisoner may kneel;
I come of those who once they write a law
Do barricade themselves against appeal.

So stand I now condemned by mine own tort;
Extenuations? There is none to plead.
I am my own most ultimate resort;
There is no pardon for the stricken Mede.
I turn to go, half valiant, half absurd,
To perish on a promise, die on a word.

Valedictory

No word upon the boarded page
That once in praise I spoke,
Would I in bitterness and rage,
Had I the power, revoke.
Take them and bind them to your heart,
With ribbon or with rue.
An end arrives to all we start;
I write no more of you.

Go then, adhere to the vows you make
Out of a haughty heart;
No more to tremble for my sake
Nor writhe beneath the smart
Of hearing on an alien tongue
Tolled lightly and in play,
The bell by which our lives were rung,
The bell we break today.

Love ever was the brightest dream
My pen might seize upon;
Think not I shall renounce the theme
Now that the dream is done.
We are put by, but not the Bow,
The Arrows, and the Dove.
Though you and I go down, still glow
The armaments of love.

The essence shines devoid of form,
Passion plucked of its sting,
The Holy Rose that hides no worm,
The Everlasting Thing.
Though loud I cry on Venus' name
To heal me and subdue
The rising tide, the raging flame,
I write no more of you.

Rare was the poem we began
(We called it that!) to live,
And for a while the measures ran
With all the heart could give.
But, oh, the golden vein was thin,
Early the dark cock crew;
The heart cried out (love's muezzin):
I write no more of you.

COLOR

To Certain Critics

Then call me traitor if you must,
Shout treason and default!
Say I betray a sacred trust
Aching beyond this vault.
I'll bear your censure as your praise,
For never shall the clan
Confine my singing to its ways
Beyond the ways of man.

No racial option narrows grief,
Pain is no patriot,
And sorrow plaits her dismal leaf
For all as lief as not.
With blind sheep groping every hill,
Searching an oriflamme,
How shall the shepherd heart then thrill
To only the darker lamb?

Black Majesty

(After reading John W. Vandercook's chronicle of sable glory)

These men were kings, albeit they were black,
Christophe and Dessalines and L'Ouverture;
Their majesty has made me turn my back
Upon a plaint I once shaped to endure.
These men were black, I say, but they were crowned
And purple-clad, however brief their time.
Stifle your agony; let grief be drowned;
We know joy had a day once and a clime.

Dark gutter-snipe, black sprawler-in-the-mud,
A thing men did a man may do again.
What answer filters through your sluggish blood
To these dark ghosts who knew so bright a reign?
"Lo, I am dark, but comely," Sheba sings.
"And we were black," three shades reply, "but kings."

Song of Praise

Who lies with his milk-white maiden,
Bound in the length of her pale gold hair,
Cooled by her lips with the cold kiss laden,
He lies, but he loves not there.

Who lies with his nut-brown maiden,
Bruised to the bone by her sin-black hair,
Warmed with the wine that her full lips trade in,
He lies, and his love lies there.

THE BLACK CHRIST

(Hopefully dedicated to White America)

The Black Christ

1

God's glory and my country's shame,
And how one man who cursed Christ's name
May never fully expiate
That crime till at the Blessed Gate
Of Heaven He meet and pardon me
Out of His love and charity;
How God, who needs no man's applause,
For love of my stark soul, of flaws
Composed, seeing it slip, did stoop
Down to the mire and pick me up,
And in the hollow of His hand
Enact again at my command
The world's supremest tragedy,
Until I die my burthen be;
How Calvary in Palestine,
Extending down to me and mine,
Was but the first leaf in a line
Of trees on which a Man should swing
World without end, in suffering
For all men's healing, let me sing.

O world grown indolent and crass,
I stand upon your bleak morass
Of incredulity and cry
Your lack of faith is but a lie.
If you but brushed the scales apart
That cloud your eyes and clinch your heart
There is no telling what grace might
Be leveled to your clearer sight;
Nor what stupendous choir break
Upon your soul till you should ache
(If you but let your fingers veer,
And raised to heaven a listening ear)
In utter pain in every limb
To know and sing as they that hymn.
If men would set their lips to prayer
With that delight with which they swear,
Heaven and earth as bow and string,
Would meet, would be attuned and sing.

We are diseased, trunk, branch, and shoot;
A sickness gathers at the root
Of us. We flaunt a gaudy fruit
But maggots wrangle at the core.
We cry for angels; yet wherefore,
Who raise no Jacobs any more? . . .
No men with eyes quick to perceive
The Shining Thing, clutch at its sleeve,
Against the strength of Heaven try
The valiant force of men who die;—
With heaving heart where courage sings
Strive with a mist of Light and Wings,

And wrestle all night long, though pressed
Be rib to rib and back to breast,
Till in the end the lofty guest
Pant, "Conquering human, be thou blest."

As once they stood white-plumed and still,
All unobserved on Dothan's hill,
Now, too, the angels, stride for stride,
Would march with us, but are denied.
Did we but let our credence sprout
As we do mockery and doubt,
Lord Christ Himself would stand revealed
In every barren, frosty field
That we misname the heart. Belief
In something more than pain and grief,
In only earth's most commonplace,
Might yet illumine every face
Of wretchedness, every blinded eye,
If from the hermitage where nigh
These thousand years the world of men
Has hemmed her in, might come again
With gracious eyes and gentle breath
The still unconquered Lady, Faith.
Two brothers have I had on earth,
One of spirit, one of sod;
My mother suckled one at birth,
One was the Son of God.

Since that befell which came to me,
Since I was singled out to be,
Upon a wheel of mockery,

The pattern of a new faith spun;
I never doubt that once the sun
For respite stopped in Gibeon,
Or that a Man I could not know
Two thousand ageless years ago,
To shape my profit by His loss,
Bought my redemption on a cross.

2

"Now spring that heals the wounds of earth
Is being born; and in her birth
The wounds of men may find a cure.
By such a thought I may endure,
And of some things be no less sure.
This is a cruel land, this South,
And bitter words to twist my mouth,
Burning my tongue down to its root,
Were easily found; but I am mute
Before the wonder of this thing:
That God should send so pure a spring,
Such grass to grow, such birds to sing,
And such small trees bravely to sprout
With timid leaves first coming out.
A land spring yearly levies on
Is gifted with God's benison.
The very odor of the loam
Fetters me here to this, my home.
The whitest lady in the town
Yonder trailing a silken gown
Is less kin to this dirt than I.
Rich mistresses with proud heads high

This dirt and I are one to them;
They flick us both from the bordered hem
Of lovely garments we supply;
But I and the dirt see just as high
As any lady cantering by.
Why should I cut this bond, my son,
This tie too taut to be undone?
This ground and I are we not one?
Has it not birthed and grown and fed me;
Yea, if you will, and also bled me?
That little patch of wizened corn
Aching and straining to be born,
May render back at some small rate
The blood and bone of me it ate.
The weevil there that rends apart
My cotton also tears my heart.
Here too, your father, lean and black,
Paid court to me with all the knack
Of any dandy in the town,
And here were born, and here have grown,
His sons and mine, as lean and black.
What ghosts there are in this old shack
Of births and deaths, soft times and hard!
I count it little being barred
From those who undervalue me.
I have my own soul's ecstasy.
Men may not bind the summer sea,
Nor set a limit to the stars;
The sun seeps through all iron bars;
The moon is ever manifest.
These things my heart always possessed.

And more than this (and here's the crown)
No man, my son, can batter down
The star-flung ramparts of the mind.
So much for flesh; I am resigned,
Whom God has made shall He not guide?"

So spake my mother, and her pride
For one small minute in its tide
Bore all my bitterness away.
I saw the thin bent form, the gray
Hair shadowed in the candlelight,
The eyes fast parting with their sight,
The rough, brown fingers, lean with toil,
Marking her kinship to the soil.
Year crowding year, after the death
Of that one man whose last drawn breath
Had been the gasping of her name,
She had wrought on, lit with some flame
Her children sensed, but could not see,
And with a patient wizardry
Wheedled her stubborn bit of land
To yield beneath her coaxing hand,
And sometimes in a lavish hour
To blossom even with a flower.
Time after time her eyes grew dim
Watching a life pay for the whim
Some master of the land must feed
To keep her people down. The seed
They planted in her children's breasts
Of hatred toward these men like beasts
She weeded out with legends how

Once there had been somewhere as now
A people harried, low in the dust;
But such had been their utter trust
In Heaven and its field of stars
That they had broken down their bars,
And walked across a parted sea
Praising His name who set them free.
I think more than the tales she told,
The music in her voice, the gold
And mellow notes she wrought,
Made us forbear to voice the thought
Low-buried underneath our love,
That we saw things she knew not of.
We had no scales upon our eyes;
God, if He was, kept to His skies,
And left us to our enemies.
Often at night fresh from our knees
And sorely doubted litanies
We grappled for the mysteries:
"We never seem to reach nowhere,"
Jim with a puzzled, questioning air,
Would kick the covers back and stare
For me the elder to explain.
As like as not, my sole refrain
Would be, "A man was lynched last night."
"Why?" Jim would ask, his eyes star-bright.
"A white man struck him; he showed fight.
Maybe God thinks such things are right."
"Maybe God never thinks at all—
Of us," and Jim would clench his small,
Hard fingers tight into a ball.

"Likely there ain't no God at all,"
Jim was the first to clothe a doubt
With words, that long had tried to sprout
Against our wills and love of one
Whose faith was like a blazing sun
Set in a dark, rebellious sky.
Now then the roots were fast, and I
Must nurture them in her despite.
God could not be, if He deemed right,
The grief that ever met our sight.

Jim grew; a brooder, silent, sheathed;
But pride was in the air he breathed;
Inside you knew an Ætna seethed.
Often when some new holocaust
Had come to undermine and blast
The life of some poor wretch we knew,
His bones would show like white scars through
His fists in anger's futile way.
"I have a fear," he used to say,
"This thing may come to me some day.
Some man contemptuous of my race
And its lost rights in this hard place,
Will strike me down for being black.
But when I answer I'll pay back
The late revenge long overdue
A thousand of my kind and hue.
A thousand black men, long since gone
Will guide my hand, stiffen the brawn,
And speed one life-divesting blow
Into some granite face of snow.

And I may swing, but not before
I send some pale ambassador
Hot footing it to hell to say
A proud black man is on his way."

When such hot venom curled his lips
And anger snapped like sudden whips
Of lightning in his eyes, her words,—
Slow, gentle as the fall of birds
That having strained to win aloft
Spread out their wings and slowly waft
Regretfully back to the earth,—
Would challenge him to name the worth
Contained in any seed of hate.
Ever the same soft words would mate
Upon her lips: love, trust, and wait.
But he, young, quick, and passionate,
Could not so readily conceal,
Deeper than acid-burns, or steel
Inflicted wounds, his vital hurt;
So still the bitter phrase would spurt:
"The things I've seen, the things I see,
Show what my neighbor thinks of me.
The world is large enough for two
Men any time, of any hue.
I give pale men a wide berth ever;
Best not to meet them, for I never
Could bend my spirit, never truckle
To them; my blood's too hot to knuckle."

And true; the neighbors spoke of him
As that proud nigger, handsome Jim.

It was a grudging compliment,
Half paid in jest, half fair intent,
By those whose partial, jaundiced eye
Saw each of us as one more fly,
Or one more bug the summer brings,
All shaped alike; antennæ, wings,
And noxious all; if caught, to die.
But Jim was not just one more fly,
For he was handsome in a way
Night is after a long, hot day.
If blood flows on from heart to heart,
And strong men leave their counterpart
In vice and virtue in their seed,
Jim's bearing spoke his imperial breed.
I was an offshoot, crude, inclined
More to the earth; he was the kind
Whose every graceful movement said,
As blood must say, by turn of head,
By twist of wrist, and glance of eye,
"Good blood flows here, and it runs high."
He had an ease of limb, a raw,
Clean, hilly stride that women saw
With quickened throbbings of the breast.
There was a show of wings; the nest
Was too confined; Jim needed space
To loop and dip and interlace;
For he had passed the stripling stage,
And stood a man, ripe for the wage
A man extorts of life; his gage
Was down. The beauty of the year
Was on him now, and somewhere near
By in the woods, as like as not,

His cares were laid away, forgot
In hearty wonderment and praise
Of one of spring's all perfect days.

But in my heart a shadow walked
At beauty's side; a terror stalked
For prey this loveliness of time.
A curse lay on this land and clime.
For all my mother's love of it,
Prosperity could not be writ
In any book of destiny
For this most red epitome
Of man's consistent cruelty
To man. Corruption, blight, and rust
Were its reward, and canker must
Set in. There were too many ghosts
Upon its lanes, too many hosts
Of dangling bodies in the wind,
Too many voices, choked and thinned,
Beseeching mercy on its air.
And like the sea set in my ear
Ever there surged the steady fear
Lest this same end and brutal fate
March toward my proud, importunate
Young brother. Often he'd say,
"'Twere best, I think, we moved away."
But custom and an unseen hand
Compelled allegiance to this land
In her, and she by staying nailed
Us there, by love securely jailed.

But love and fear must end their bout,
And one or both be counted out.
Rebellion barked now like a gun;
Like a split dam, this faith in one
Who in my sight had never done
One extraordinary thing
That I should praise his name, or sing
His bounty and his grace, let loose
The pent-up torrent of abuse
That clamored in me for release:
"Nay, I have done with deities
Who keep me ever on my knees,
My mouth forever in a tune
Of praise, yet never grant the boon
Of what I pray for night and day.
God is a toy; put Him away.
Or make you one of wood or stone
That you can call your very own,
A thing to feel and touch and stroke,
Who does not break you with a yoke
Of iron that he whispers soft;
Nor promise you fine things aloft
While back and belly here go bare,
While His own image walks so spare
And finds this life so hard to live
You doubt that He has aught to give.
Better an idol shaped of clay
Near you, than one so far away.
Although it may not heed your labors,
At least it will not mind your neighbors'.
'In His own time, He will unfold

You milk and honey, streets of gold,
High walls of jasper . . .' phrases rolled
Upon the tongues of idiots.
What profit *then*, if hunger gluts
Us *now*? Better my God should be
This moving, breathing frame of me,
Strong hands and feet, live heart and eyes;
And when these cease, say then God dies.
Your God is somewhere worlds away
Hunting a star He shot astray;
Oh, He has weightier things to do
Than lavish time on me and you.
What thought has He of us, three motes
Of breath, three scattered notes
In His grand symphony, the world?
Once we were blown, once we were hurled
In place, we were as soon forgot.
He might not linger on one dot
When there were bars and staves to fling
About, for waiting stars to sing.
When Rome was a suckling, when Greece was young,
Then there were Gods fit to be sung,
Who paid the loyal devotee
For service rendered zealously,
In coin a man might feel and spend,
Not marked 'Deferred to Journey's End.'
The servant then was worth his hire;
He went unscathed through flood and fire;
Gods were a thing then to admire.
'Bow down and worship us,' they said.
'You shall be clothed, be housed and fed,

While yet you live, not when you're dead.
Strong are our arms where yours are weak.
On them that harm you will we wreak
The vengeance of a God though they
Were Gods like us in every way.
Not merely is an honor laid
On those we touch with our accolade;
We strike for you with that same blade!'"
My mother shook a weary head—
"Visions are not for all," she said,
"There were no risings from the dead,
No frightened quiverings of earth
To mark my spirit's latter birth.
The light that on Damascus' road
Blinded a scoffer never glowed
For me. I had no need to view
His side, or pass my fingers through
Christ's wounds. It breaks like that on some,
And yet it can as surely come
Without the lightning and the rain.
Some who must have their hurricane
Go stumbling through it for a light
They never find. Only the night
Of doubt is opened to their sight.
They weigh and measure, search, define,—
But he who seeks a thing divine
Must humbly lay his lore aside,
And like a child believe; confide
In Him whose ways are deep and dark,
And in the end perhaps the spark
He sought will be revealed. Perchance

Some things are hard to countenance,
And others difficult to probe;
But shall the mind that grew this globe,
And out of chaos thought a world,
To us be totally unfurled?
And all we fail to comprehend,
Shall such a mind be asked to bend
Down to, unravel, and untwine?
If those who highest hold His sign,
Who praise Him most with loudest tongue
Are granted no high place among
The crowd, shall we be bitter then?
The puzzle shall grow simple when
The soul discards the ways of dust.
There is no gain in doubt; but trust
Is our one magic wand. Through it
We and eternity are knit,
Death made a myth, and darkness lit.
The slave can meet the monarch's gaze
With equal pride, dreaming to days
When slave and monarch both shall be,
Transmuted everlastingly,
A single reed blown on to sing
The glory of the only King."

We had not, in the stealthy gloom
Of deepening night, that shot our room
With queerly capering shadows through,
Noticed the form that wavered to
And fro on weak, unsteady feet
Within the door; I turned to greet

Spring's gayest cavalier, but Jim
Who stood there balanced in the dim
Half-light waved me away from him.
And then I saw how terror streaked
His eyes, and how a red flow leaked
And slid from cheek to chin. His hand
Still grasped a knotted branch, and spanned
It fiercely, fondling it. At last
He moved into the light, and cast
His eyes about, as if to wrap
In one soft glance, before the trap
Was sprung, all he saw mirrored there:
All love and bounty; grace; all fair,
All discontented days; sweet weather;
Rain-slant, snow-fall; all things together
Which any man about to die
Might ask to have filmed on his eye,
And then he bowed his haughty head,
"The thing we feared has come," he said;
"But put your ear down to the ground,
And you may hear the deadly sound
Of two-limbed dogs that bay for me.
If any ask in time to be
Why I was parted from my breath,
Here is your tale: I went to death
Because a man murdered the spring.
Tell them though they dispute this thing,
This is the song that dead men sing:
One spark of spirit Godhead gave
To all alike, to sire and slave,
From earth's red core to each white pole,

This one identity of soul;
That when the pipes of beauty play,
The feet must dance, the limbs must sway,
And even the heart with grief turned lead,
Beauty shall lift like a leaf wind-sped,
Shall swoop upon in gentle might,
Shall toss and tease and leave so light
That never again shall grief or care
Find long or willing lodgement there.
Tell them each law and rule they make
Mankind shall disregard and break
(If this must be) for beauty's sake.
Tell them what pranks the spring can play;
The young colt leaps, the cat that lay
In a sullen ball all winter long
Breaks like a kettle into song;
Waving it high like a limber flail,
The kitten worries his own brief tail;
While man and dog sniff the wind alike,
For the new smell hurts them like a spike
Of steel thrust quickly through the breast;
Earth heaves and groans with a sharp unrest.

The poet, though he sang of death,
Finds tunes for music in simple breath;
Even the old, the sleepy-eyed,
Are stirred to movement by the tide.
But oh, the young, the aging young,
Spring is a sweetmeat to our tongue;
Spring is the paean; we the choir;
Spring is the fuel; we the fire.
Tell them spring's feathery weight will jar,

Though it were iron, any bar
Upreared by men to keep apart
Two who when probed down to the heart
Speak each a common tongue. Tell them
Two met, each stooping to the hem
Of beauty passing by. Such awe
Grew on them hate began to thaw
And fear and dread to melt and run
Like ice laid siege to by the sun.
Say for a moment's misty space
These had forgotten hue and race;
Spring blew too loud and green a blast
For them to think on rank and caste.
The homage they both understood,
(Taught on a bloody Christless rood)
Due from his dark to her brighter blood,
In such an hour, at such a time,
When all their world was one clear rhyme,
He could not give, nor she exact.
This only was a glowing fact:
Spring in a green and golden gown,
And feathered feet, had come to town;
Spring in a rich habiliment
That shook the breath and woke the spent
And sleepy pulse to a dervish beat,
Spring had the world again at her feet.
Spring was a lady fair and rich,
And they were fired with the season's itch
To hold her train or stroke her hair
And tell her shyly they found her fair.
Spring was a voice so high and clear

It broke their hearts as they leaned to hear
In stream and grass and soft bird's-wing;
Spring was in them and they were spring.
Then say, a smudge across the day,
A bit of crass and filthy clay,
A blot of ink upon a white
Page in a book of gold; a tight
Curled worm hid in the festive rose,
A mind so foul it hurt your nose,
Came one of earth's serene elect,
His righteous being warped and flecked
With what his thoughts were: stench and smut. . . .
I had gone on unheeding but
He struck me down, he called her slut,
And black man's mistress, bawdy whore,
And such like names, and many more,—
(Christ, what has spring to answer for!)
I had gone on, I had been wise,
Knowing my value in those eyes
That seared me through and out and in,
Finding a thing to taunt and grin
At in my hair and hue. My right
I knew could not outweigh his might
Who had the law for satellite—
Only I turned to look at her,
The early spring's first worshiper,
(Spring, what have you to answer for?)
The blood had fled from either cheek
And from her lips; she could not speak,
But she could only stand and stare
And let her pain stab through the air.

I think a blow to heart or head
Had hurt her less than what he said.
A blow can be so quick and kind,
But words will feast upon the mind
And gnaw the heart down to a shred,
And leave you living, yet leave you dead.
If he had only tortured me,
I could have borne it valiantly.
The things he said in littleness
Were cheap, the blow he dealt me less,
Only they totalled more; he gagged
And bound a spirit there; he dragged
A sunlit gown of gold and green,—
(The season's first, first to be seen)
And feathered feet, and a plumèd hat,—
(First of the year to be wondered at)
Through muck and mire, and by the hair
He caught a lady rich and fair.
His vile and puny fingers churned
Our world about that sang and burned
A while as never world before.
He had unlatched an icy door,
And let the winter in once more.
To kill a man is a woeful thing,
But he who lays a hand on spring,
Clutches the first bird by its throat
And throttles it in the midst of a note;
Whose breath upon the leaf-proud tree
Turns all that wealth to penury;
Whose touch upon the first shy flower
Gives it a blight before its hour;

Whose craven face above a pool
That otherwise were clear and cool,
Transforms that running silver dream
Into a hot and sluggish stream
Thus better fit to countenance
His own corrupt unhealthy glance,
Of all men is most infamous;
His deed is rank and blasphemous.
The erstwhile warm, the short time sweet,
Spring now lay frozen at our feet.
Say then, why say nothing more
Except I had to close the door;
And this man's leer loomed in the way.
The air began to sting; then say
There was this branch; I struck; he fell;
There's holiday, I think, in hell."

Outside the night began to groan
As heavy feet crushed twig and stone
Beating a pathway to our door;
A thin noise first, and then a roar
More animal than human grew
Upon the air until we knew
No mercy could be in the sound.
"Quick, hide," I said. I glanced around;
But no abyss gaped in the ground.
But in the eyes of fear a twig
Will seem a tree, a straw as big
To him who drowns as any raft.
So being mad, being quite daft,
I shoved him in a closet set

Against the wall. This would but let
Him breathe two minutes more, or three,
Before they dragged him out to be
Queer fruit upon some outraged tree.
Our room was in a moment lit
With flaring brands; men crowded it—
Old men whose eyes were better sealed
In sleep; strong men with muscles steeled
Like rods, whose place was in the field;
Striplings like Jim with just a touch
Of down upon the chin; for such
More fitting a secluded hedge
To lie beneath with one to pledge
In youth's hot words, immortal love.
These things they were not thinking of;
"Lynch him! Lynch him!" O savage cry,
Why should you echo, "Crucify!"
One sought, sleek-tongued, to pacify
Them with slow talk of trial, law,
Established court; the dripping maw
Would not be wheedled from its prey.
Out of the past I heard him say,
"So be it then; have then your way;
But not by me shall blood be spilt;
I wash my hands clean of this guilt."
This was an echo of a phrase
Uttered how many million days
Gone by?
      Water may cleanse the hands
But what shall scour the soul that stands
Accused in heaven's sight?

"The Kid."

One cried, "Where is the bastard hid?"
"He is not here."

It was a faint

And futile lie.

"The hell he ain't;

We tracked him here. Show us the place,
Or else . . ."

He made an ugly face,

Raising a heavy club to smite.
I had been felled, had not the sight
Of all been otherwise arraigned.
Each with bewilderment unfeigned
Stared hard to see against the wall
The hunted boy stand slim and tall;
Dream-born, it seemed, with just a trace
Of weariness upon his face,
He stood as if evolved from air;
As if always he had stood there. . . .
What blew the torches' feeble flare
To such a soaring fury now?
Each hand went up to fend each brow,
Save his; he and the light were one,
A man by night clad with the sun.
By form and feature, bearing, name,
I knew this man. He was the same
Whom I had thrust, a minute past,
Behind a door,—and made it fast.
Knit flesh and bone, had like a thong,
Bound us as one our whole life long,
But in the presence of this throng,

He seemed one I had never known.
Never such tragic beauty shone
As this on any face before.
It pared the heart straight to the core.
It is the lustre dying lends,
I thought, to make some brief amends
To life so wantonly cut down.
The air about him shaped a crown
Of light, or so it seemed to me,
And sweeter than the melody
Of leaves in rain, and far more sad,
His voice descended on the mad,
Blood-sniffing crowd that sought his life,
A voice where grief cut like a knife:
"I am he whom you seek, he whom
You will not spare his daily doom.
My march is ever to the tomb,
But let the innocent go free;
This man and woman, let them be,
Who loving much have succored me."
And then he turned about to speak
To me whose heart was fit to break,
"My brother, when this wound has healed,
And you reap in some other field
Roses, and all a spring can yield;
Brother (to call me so!) then prove
Out of your charity and love
That I was not unduly slain,
That this my death was not in vain.
For no life should go to the tomb
Unless from it a new life bloom,

A greater faith, a clearer sight,
A wiser groping for the light."
He moved to where our mother stood,
Dry-eyed, though grief was at its flood,
"Mother, not poorer losing one,
Look now upon your dying son."
Her own life trembling on the brim,
She raised woe-ravaged eyes to him,
And in their glances something grew
And spread, till healing fluttered through
Her pain, a vision so complete
It sent her humbly to his feet
With what I deemed a curious cry,
"And must this be for such as I?"
Even his captors seemed to feel
Disquietude, an unrest steal
Upon their ardor, dampening it,
Till one less fearful varlet hit
Him across the mouth a heavy blow,
Drawing a thin, yet steady flow
Of red to drip a dirge of slow
Finality upon my heart.
The end came fast. Given the start
One hound must always give the pack
That fears the meekest prey whose back
Is desperate against a wall,
They charged. I saw him stagger, fall
Beneath a mill of hands, feet, staves.
And I like one who sees huge waves
In hunger rise above the skiff
At sea, yet watching from a cliff

Far off can lend no feeblest aid,
No more than can a fragile blade
Of grass in some far distant land,
That has no heart to wrench, nor hand
To stretch in vain, could only stand
With streaming eyes and watch the play.

There grew a tree a little way
Off from the hut, a virgin tree
Awaiting its fecundity.
O Tree was ever worthier Groom
Led to a bride of such rare bloom?
Did ever fiercer hands enlace
Love and Beloved in an embrace
As heaven-smiled-upon as this?
Was ever more celestial kiss?
But once, did ever anywhere
So full a choir chant such an air
As feathered splendors bugled there?
And was there ever blinder eye
Or deafer ear than mine?
                              A cry
So soft, and yet so brimming filled
With agony, my heart strings thrilled
An ineffectual reply,—
Then gaunt against the southern sky
The silent handiwork of hate.
Greet, Virgin Tree, your holy mate!

No sound then in the little room
Was filtered through my sieve of gloom,

Except the steady fall of tears,
The hot, insistent rain that sears
The burning ruts down which it goes,
The futile flow, for all one knows
How vain it is, that ever flows.
I could not bear to look at *her*
There in the dark; I could not stir
From where I sat, so weighted down.
The king of grief, I held my crown
So dear, I wore my tattered gown
With such affection and such love
That though I strove I could not move.
But I could hear (and this unchained
The raging beast in me) her pained
And sorrow-riven voice ring out
Above the spirit's awful rout,
Above the howling winds of doubt,
How she knew Whom she traveled to
Was judge of all that men might do
To such as she who trusted Him.
Faith was a tower for her, grim
And insurmountable; and death
She said was only changing breath
Into an essence fine and rare.
Anger smote me and most despair
Seeing her still bow down in prayer.
"Call on Him now," I mocked, "and try
Your faith against His deed, while I
With intent equally as sane,
Searching a motive for this pain,
Will hold a little stone on high

And seek of it the reason why.
Which, stone or God, will first reply?
Why? Hear me ask it. He was young
And beautiful. Why was he flung
Like common dirt to death? Why, stone,
Must he of all the earth atone
For what? The dirt God used was homely
But the man He made was comely.
What child creating out of sand,
With puckered brow and intent hand,
Would see the lovely thing he planned
Struck with a lewd and wanton blade,
Nor stretch a hand to what he made,
Nor shed a childish, futile tear,
Because he loved it, held it dear?
Would not a child's weak heart rebel?
But Christ who conquered Death and Hell
What has He done for you who spent
A bleeding life for His content?
Or is the white Christ, too, distraught
By these dark sins His Father wrought?"

I mocked her so until I broke
Beneath my passion's heavy yoke.
My world went black with grief and pain;
My very bitterness was slain,
And I had need of only sleep,
Or some dim place where I might weep
My life away, some misty haunt
Where never man might come to taunt
Me with the thought of how men scar

Their brothers here, or what we are
Upon this most accursèd star.
Not that sweet sleep from which some wake
All fetterless, without an ache
Of heart or limb, but such a sleep
As had raped him, eternal, deep;—
Deep as my woe, vast as my pain,
Sleep of the young and early-slain.
My Lycidas was dead. There swung
In all his glory, lusty, young,
My Jonathan, my Patrocles,
(For with his death there perished these)
And I had neither sword nor song,
Only an acid-bitten tongue,
Fit neither in its poverty
For vengeance nor for threnody,
Only for tears and blasphemy.

Now God be praised that a door should creak,
And that a rusty hinge should shriek.
Of all sweet sounds that I may hear
Of lute or lyre or dulcimer,
None ever shall assail my ear
Sweet as the sound of a grating door
I had thought closed forevermore.
Out of my deep-ploughed agony,
I turned to see a door swing free;
The very door he once came through
To death, now framed for us anew
His vital self, his and no other's
Live body of the dead, my brother's.

Like one who dreams within a dream,
Hand at my throat, lest I should scream,
I moved with hopeful, doubting pace
To meet the dead man face to face.

"Bear witness now unto His grace";
I heard my mother's mounting word,
"Behold the glory of the Lord,
His unimpeachable high seal.
Cry mercy now before Him; kneel,
And let your heart's conversion swell
The wonder of His miracle."

I saw; I touched; yet doubted him;
My fingers faltered down his slim
Sides, down his breathing length of limb.
Incredulous of sight and touch,
"No more," I cried, "this is too much
For one mad brain to stagger through."
For there he stood in utmost view
Whose death I had been witness to;
But now he breathed; he lived; he walked;
His tongue could speak my name; he talked.
He questioned me to know what art
Had made his enemies depart.
Either I leaped or crawled to where
I last had seen stiff on the air
The form than life more dear to me;
But where had swayed that misery
Now only was a flowering tree
That soon would travail into fruit.

Slowly my mind released its mute
Bewilderment, while truth took root
In me and blossomed into light:
"Down, down," I cried, in joy and fright,
As all He said came back to me
With what its true import must be,
"Upon our knees and let the worst,
Let me the sinfullest kneel first;
O lovely Head to dust brought low
More times than we can ever know
Whose small regard, dust-ridden eye,
Behold Your doom, yet doubt You die;
O Form immaculately born,
Betrayed a thousand times each morn,
As many times each night denied,
Surrendered, tortured, crucified!
Now have we seen beyond degree
That love which has no boundary;
Our eyes have looked on Calvary."

No sound then in the sacred gloom
That blessed the shrine that was our room
Except the steady rise of praise
To Him who shapes all nights and days
Into one final burst of sun;
Though with the praise some tears must run
In pity of the King's dear breath
That ransomed one of us from death.

The days are mellow for us now;
We reap full fields; the heavy bough

Bends to us in another land;
The ripe fruit falls into our hand.
My mother, Job's dark sister, sits
Now in a corner, prays, and knits.
Often across her face there flits
Remembered pain, to mar her joy,
At Whose death gave her back her boy.
While I who mouthed my blasphemies,
Recalling now His agonies,
Am found forever on my knees,
Ever to praise her Christ with her,
Knowing He can at will confer
Magic on miracle to prove
And try me when I doubt His love.
If I am blind He does not see;
If I am lame He halts with me;
There is no hood of pain I wear
That has not rested on His hair
Making Him first initiate
Beneath its harsh and hairy weight.
He grew with me within the womb;
He will receive me at the tomb.
He will make plain the misty path
He makes me tread in love and wrath,
And bending down in peace and grace
May wear again my brother's face.

Somewhere the Southland rears a tree,
(And many others there may be
Like unto it, that are unknown,
Whereon as costly fruit has grown).

It stands before a hut of wood
In which the Christ Himself once stood—
And those who pass it by may see
Nought growing there except a tree,
But there are two to testify
Who hung on it . . . we saw Him die.
Its roots were fed with priceless blood.
It is the Cross; it is the Rood.

Paris, January 31, 1929

THE MEDEA AND SOME POEMS | 1935

After a Visit

(At Padraic Colum's where there were Irish poets)

Last night I lay upon my bed and would have slept;
But all around my head was wet with tears I wept,
As bitter dreams swarmed in like bees to sting my brain,
While others kissed like endless snakes forged in a chain,
Dull-eyed Eumenides estranging me and sleep,
Each soft insidious caress biting me deep.
And I wept not what I had done but what let go,
Between two seasons, one of fire and one of snow.
I had known joy and sorrow I had surely known,
But out of neither any piercing note was blown.
Friends had been kind and surely friends had faithless
      been,
But long ago my heart was closed, panelled within.
And I had walked two seasons through, and moved
      among
Strange ways and folk, and all the while no line was
      wrung
In praise or blame of aught from my frost-bitten tongue.
Silence had sunned me with her hot, embalming mouth,
And indolence had watered me with drops of drouth.
Then I walked in a room where Irish poets were;
I saw the muse enthroned, heard how they worshiped her,

Felt men nor gods could ever so envenom them
That Poetry could pass and they not grasp her hem,
Not cry on her for healing; shaken off, still praise,
Not questioning her enigmatical delays.
And shame of my apostasy was like a coal
That reached my tongue and heart and far off frigid
    soul,
Melting myself into myself, making me weep
Regeneration's burning tears, preluding sleep.

Magnets

The straight, the swift, the debonair,
Are targets on the thoroughfare
For every kind appraising eye;
Sweet words are said as they pass by.
But such a strange contrary thing
My heart is, it will never cling
To any bright unblemished thing.
Such have their own security,
And little need to lean on me.
The limb that falters in its course,
And cries, "Not yet!" to waning force;
The orb that may not brave the sun;
The bitter mouth, its kissing done;
The loving heart that must deny
The very love it travels by;
What most has need to bend and pray,
These magnets draw my heart their way.

Any Human to Another

The ills I sorrow at
Not me alone
Like an arrow,
Pierce to the marrow,
Through the fat
And past the bone.

Your grief and mine
Must intertwine
Like sea and river,
Be fused and mingle,
Diverse yet single,
Forever and forever.

Let no man be so proud
And confident,
To think he is allowed
A little tent
Pitched in a meadow
Of sun and shadow
All his little own.

Joy may be shy, unique,
Friendly to a few,
Sorrow never scorned to speak
To any who
Were false or true.

Your every grief
Like a blade
Shining and unsheathed
Must strike me down.
Of bitter aloes wreathed,
My sorrow must be laid
On your head like a crown.

Only the Polished Skeleton

The heart has need of some deceit
    To make its pistons rise and fall;
For less than this it would not beat,
    Nor flush the sluggish vein at all.

With subterfuge and fraud the mind
    Must fend and parry thrust for thrust,
With logic brutal and unkind
    Beat off the onslaughts of the dust.

Only the polished skeleton,
    Of flesh relieved and pauperized,
Can rest at ease and think upon
    The worth of all it so despised.

Every Lover

There were no lovers bowed before my time;
Before this treachery was none betrayed;
No blown heart pricked and thinned; drained as a lime;
Interred beyond the skill of pick or spade.
Mine is the first that like an egg Love sucks,—
Sly Love the weasel, Love the fox, the asp,
Love wearing any guise that rends or plucks,
Slits with hid fang, binds with a golden clasp.
This pain is my sore heart's unique distress,
An alien humour to the common brood,
Invading once in time our littleness,
Mingling a god's disease with mortal blood.
Surely this visitation is divine;
No breast has fed a malady like mine.

To France

Though I am not the first in English terms
To name you of the earth's great nations Queen;
Though better poets chant it to the worms
How that fair city perched upon the Seine
Is lovelier than that they traveled to;
While kings and warriors and many a priest
In their last hour have smiled to think of you,
Among these count me not the last nor least.

As he whose eyes are gouged craves light to see,
And he whose limbs are broken strength to run,
So have I sought in you that alchemy
That knits my bones and turns me to the sun;
And found across a continent of foam
What was denied my hungry heart at home.

Sleep

Nothing is lovelier than sleep,
Nor kinder thing was ever made;
Gently, as though a cat should creep
Upon a bird, transfixed, way-laid,
It sinks in us its velvet blade.

Soft are those paws, if they are sheathed,
The steel of troubling dreams withdrawn,
And all in peace lapped round and wreathed
The mind sinks down as on a lawn
Laid out between the dusk and dawn.

That dark maternal fountain bared
To give her weakest creature food,
The bosom of the Night is shared
By all her weary, stricken brood;
And though the suck be short, 'tis good.

Speed then that longer, darker eve,
Which heavy dream nor light shall break,
Nor Day's white sword pierce through and grieve,
Where Death's full bosom bids us take,
And every thirst we knew to slake.

Medusa

I mind me how when first I looked at her
A warning shudder in the blood cried, "Ware!
Those eyes are basilisk's she gazes through,
And those are snakes you take for strands of hair!"
But I was never one to be subdued
By any fear of aught not reason-bred,
And so I mocked the ruddy word, and stood
To meet the gold-envenomed dart instead.

O vengeful warning, spiteful stream, a truce!
What boots this constant crying in the wind,
This ultimate indignity: abuse
Heaped on a tree of all its foliage thinned?
Though blind, yet on these arid balls engraved
I know it was a lovely face I braved.

Interlude

Now I am cooled of folly's heat,
   My tides are at an ebb,
And I no longer find it sweet
   To play fly to your web.

Now I have back my heart again,
   My feet have sprouted wings;
My tongue imprisoned long in pain
   Unlocks itself and sings.

Three Nonsense Rhymes for My Three Goddaughters

1   *For Diana*

The king of Spain had seven daughters,
Six white as snow, one black as jet;
All day they pranked where Spanish waters
Spumed up a silver parapet.
The king of Spain and his seven daughters,
Six white as snow, one black as jet,
Are dust beneath the Spanish waters
Whose silver streams are playing yet.

2   *For Barbara who seldom smiles*

People who are gracious,
People who are kind,
I let explore the alleys,
The mountains and the valleys,
That pattern up my mind.

For people who are haughty,
And people who are proud,
I spread a net, and once they're caught,
I lock them up within a thought
I never think aloud.

3   *Mathematics for Carol not yet two*
Up is up
And down is down
And round is all about,
But how far in
Our wisdom goes
We haven't yet found out.

Sonnet

I have not loved you in the noblest way
The human heart can beat, where what it loves
Is canonized and purged, outtops the day
To masquerade beneath itself,—as gloves
Upon a pilfering hand (sly fingers) laid,
Can make them move as something frank and kind,—
Yet in the curved-up palm is niched a blade;
Loved have I much, but I have not been blind.

The noblest way is fraught with too much pain;
Who travels it must drag a crucifix;
What hurts my heart hurts deep and to the grain;
My mother never dipped me in the Styx,
And who would find me weak and vulnerable
Need never aim his arrow at my heel.

Sonnet

Some for a little while do love, and some for long;
And some rare few forever and for aye;
Some for the measure of a poet's song,
And some the ribbon width of a summer's day.
Some on a golden crucifix do swear,
And some in blood do plight a fickle troth;
Some struck divinely mad may only stare,
And out of silence weave an iron oath.

So many ways love has none may appear
The bitter best, and none the sweetest worst;
Strange food the hungry have been known to bear,
And brackish water slakes an utter thirst.
It is a rare and tantalizing fruit
Our hands reach for, but nothing absolute.

Sonnet

I know now how a man whose blood is hot
And rich, still undiminished of desire,
Thinking (too soon), "The world is dust and mire,"
Must feel who takes to wife four walls, a cot,
A hempen robe and cowl, saying, "I'll not
To anything, save God and Heaven's fire,
Permit a thought; and I will never tire
Of Christ, and in Him all shall be forgot."

He too, as it were Torquemada's rack,
Writhes piteously on that unyielding bed,
Crying, "Take Heaven all, but give me back
Those words and sighs without which I am dead;
Which thinking on are lances, and I reel."
Letting you go, I know how he would feel.

To One Not There

(For D. W.)

This is a land in which you never were,
A land perchance which you may never see;
And yet the length of it I may not stir,
But your sweet spirit walks its ways with me.
Your voice is in these Gallic accents light,
And sweeter is the Rhenish wine I sip
Because this glass (a lesser Grail) is bright
Illumined by the memory of your lip.

Thus would I have it in the dismal day,
When I fare forth upon another ship,
The heart not warm as now; but cold, and clay;
The journey forced; not, sweet, a pleasure trip.
Thus would I take your image by the hand,
But leave you safe within a living land.

Paris, July 1933

Sonnet

What I am saying now was said before,
And countless centuries from now again,
Some poet warped with bitterness and pain,
Will brew like words hoping to salve his sore.
And seeing written he will think the core
Of anguish from that throbbing wound, his brain,
Squeezed out; and these ill humours gone, disdain,
Or think he does, the face he loved of yore.

And then he too, as I, will turn to look
Upon his instrument of discontent,
Thinking himself a Perseus, and fit to brook
Her columned throat and every blandishment;
And looking know what brittle arms we wield,
Whose pencil is our sword, whose page our shield.

Sonnet

These are no wind-blown rumors, soft say-sos,
No garden-whispered hearsays, lightly heard:
I know that summer never spares the rose,
That spring is faithless to the brightest bird.
I know that nothing lovely shall prevail
To win from Time and Death a moment's grace;
At Beauty's birth the scythe was honed, the nail
Dipped for her hands, the cowl clipped for her face.

And yet I cannot think that this my faith,
My wingèd joy, my pride, my utmost mirth,
Centered in you, shall ever taste of death,
Or perish from the false, forgetting earth.
You are with time, as wind and weather are,
As is the sun, and every nailèd star.

Sonnet Dialogue

I to My Soul:
Why this preoccupation, soul, with Death,
This servile genuflexion to the worm,
Making the tomb a Mecca where the breath
(Though still it rises vaporous, but firm,
Expelled from lungs still clear and unimpaired,
To plough through nostrils quivering with pride)
Veers in distress and love, as if it dared
Not search a gayer place, and there subside?

My Soul to Me:
Because the worm shall tread the lion down,
And in the end shall sicken at its feast,
And for a worm of even less renown
Loom as a dread but subjugated beast;
Because whatever lives is granted breath
But by the grace and sufferance of Death.

Sonnet

I would I could, as other poets have,
As some have done in happiness and pride,
Upraise a monument to love: a grave
Is what is meet to dig for what has died.
I would I could outsing, as others do,
Whatever bird has pinions to employ,
Dispute with what is heaven-born its blue,
And, lacking wings, rise on my very joy.

I would I might exchange this draggled plume
For one more exquisite, more brightly hued,
Snatched from a breast still singing in its doom,
With that unvanquished carol still endued.
But I can only sing of what I know,
And all I know, or ever knew, is woe.

Sonnet

Some things incredible I still believe,
Not having seen yet testify them true,
As verities caught in the mind's quick sieve
Too fine and beautiful to trickle through:
That somewhere lifting up his polished horn,
While on his milky flanks the sun's hot glare
Is cooled into a kiss, the Unicorn
Exists, a beast from fable wrenched apart,
One with the Phoenix and Leviathan.

Yet doubt of this so near me shakes my heart
As myth nor saga never has nor can:
That you are worth these mighty aches I bear,
This wound on wound, this tear on scalding tear.

Sonnet

Be with me, Pride; now Love is gone, stay by;
Let me nought hear but your metallic tone,
With nothing gaze but your unflinching eye.
Uplift me, Pride; compel the listless bone.
The inert hand, the brain that still would think
Upon its hurt, and most on that which gave
The wound; be my clear fountain whence I drink
Travail and toil from now until the grave.
Cling to me, leeches pinned on either hand,
As to a horse the reins he cannot shake,
Which bid him go, and go he must; or stand,
And though he strive there is no step to take.
Be stronger than this heart lest in defeat
I cast you down at her dear cloven feet.

Sonnet

Although I name you not that those who read
May point you out among the shifting crowd,
Saying, "'Tis she has made the poet bleed,

And bowed him down who might have walked so proud";
Although my heart if spliced and opened bare,
In suffering would still conceal your name,
Its redness rising up, discoloring there
All clue to you who are the utmost blame
For this my bitter living, which is death,
I am content in this: when your eyes fall
Upon these words protesting underneath,
They shall, as they were written to, recall
Your cruelty, my pain, and make you know
The hidden depths of an immortal woe.

To France

I have a dream of where (when I grow old,
Having no further joy to take in lip
Or limb, a graybeard caching from the cold
The frail indignity of age) some ship
Might bear my creaking, unhinged bones
Trailing remembrance as a tattered cloak,
And beach me glad, though on their sharpest stones,
Among a fair and kindly foreign folk.

There might I only breathe my latest days,
With those rich accents falling on my ear
That most have made me feel that freedom's rays
Still have a shrine where they may leap and sear,—
Though I were palsied there, or halt, or blind,
So I were there, I think I should not mind.

Bilitis Sings

(*From the French of Pierre Louÿs*)

Some women's charms are sheathed in wool,
   And some in silk and gold;
Some few with flowers are garlanded,
   And some green leaves enfold.

I could not live so falsely plumed;
   My lover, here I stand,
Unrobed, unjewelled, sandalless,
   But lovely to command.

The black of my hair is from no dye,
   The red of my lips is theirs;
My feathery curls float free and long,
   Unvexed by knife or shears.

Then take me as my mother shaped me
   In simple love and homely,
And if I please you so, my lover,
   Remember praise is comely.

Death to the Poor

(*From the French of Baudelaire*)

In death alone is what consoles; and life
And all its end is death; and that fond hope
Whose music like a mad fantastic fife

Compels us up this ridged and rocky slope.
Through lightning, hail, and hurt of human look,
Death is the vibrant light we travel toward,
The mystic Inn forepromised in the Book
Where all are welcomed in to bed and board.

An angel whose star-banded fingers hold
The gift of dreams and calm, ecstatic sleep
In easier beds than those we had before,
Death is the face of God, the only fold
That pens content and ever-happy sheep,
To Paradise the only open door.

The Cat

(*From the French of Baudelaire*)

Come, lovely cat, to this adoring breast;
Over thy daggers silken scabbards draw;
Into thy beauty let me plunge to rest,
Unmindful of thy swift and cruel claw.
The while my fingers leisurely caress
Thy head and vaulted back's elastic arch,
And through each tip mysterious pleasures press
And crackle on their swift dynamic march,
I see revived in thee, felinely cast,
A woman with thine eyes, satanic beast,
Profound and cold as scythes to mow me down.
And from her feet up to her throat are massed
Strange aromas; a perfume from the East
Swims round her body, sinuous and brown.

Cats

(*From the French of Baudelaire*)

Lovers that burn and learnèd scholars cold
Dote equally in their appointed time
On subtle cats which do them both combine—
Quiet as scholars and as lovers bold.
Friendly alike to sage and sybarite,
They thrive on silence; shadow is their friend;
Earth's fittest runners for the Prince of Night,
Unto no other pride their own will bend.

In noble attitudes they sit and dream,
Small sphinxes miming those in lonelier lands,
In stony sleep eternal and afar.
With passion's seed their fruitful bodies teem,
While golden scintilla like burning sands
Their eyes with mystery and light bestar.

Scottsboro, Too, Is Worth Its Song

(*A poem to American poets*)

I said:
Now will the poets sing,—
Their cries go thundering
Like blood and tears
Into the nation's ears,
Like lightning dart
Into the nation's heart.

Against disease and death and all things fell,
And war,
Their strophes rise and swell
To jar
The foe smug in his citadel.

Remembering their sharp and pretty
Tunes for Sacco and Vanzetti,
I said:
Here too's a cause divinely spun
For those whose eyes are on the sun,
Here in epitome
Is all disgrace
And epic wrong,
Like wine to brace
The minstrel heart, and blare it into song.

Surely, I said,
Now will the poets sing.
     But they have raised no cry.
     I wonder why.

The Wakeupworld

This was the song of the Wakeupworld,
The beautiful beast with long tail curled:

"Wake up, O World; O World, awake!
The light is bright on hill and lake;
O World, awake; wake up, O World!
The flags of the wind are all unfurled;
Wake up, O World; O World, awake!
Of earth's delightfulness partake.

Wake up, O World, whatever hour;
Sweet are the fields, sweet is the flower!
Wake up, O World; O World, awake;
Perhaps to see the daylight break,
Perhaps to see the sun descend,
The night begin, the daylight end.

But something surely to behold,
Not bought with silver or with gold,
Not shown in any land of dreams.
For open eyes the whole world teems
With lovely things to do or make,
Wake up, O World; O World, awake!"

Such was the song of the Wakeupworld,
The beautiful beast with long tail curled,
The Wakeupworld so swift and fleet,
With twelve bright eyes and six strong feet.
Such was the song he sang all day,
Lest man or beast should sleep away
The gift of Time, and never know
The beauties of this life below.
Twelve were his eyes, as I have said,
Placed clockwise in his massive head.
Never in any time or weather
Were all those eyes shut tight together,
But daily, at its certain hour,
Each eye became possessed of power.

At one, an eye all pale and white
Flew open for the day's first sight,
And looked alone, until at two
There woke his wondering eye of blue.
His eye of green at stroke of three
Blazed like a jewel brilliantly;
At four he opened up the red,
And all around its lustre spread.
Shyly then, as if all sleepy yet,
At five peeped forth the violet.
An eye of silver, chill and cold,
The hour of six would then unfold.
At seven with a sudden wink,
He would let loose his eye of pink.
At eight an eye so mild and mellow
Would gaze about; this one was yellow.

Prompt at the stroke of nine they say
Would twinkle forth his eye of gray.
At ten, as merry as a clown,
You could behold the laughing brown.
Eleven strikes! And open flies
An eye as black as midnight skies.
And when the hour of twelve was tolled,
And Time was one more half day old,
He opened full his eye of gold.
His twelve bright eyes he flashed around
Till rainbows flecked the trees and ground!
Oh, loveliest beast in song or story,
The Wakeupworld in all his glory!

He could not sleep as others could;
But for a moment in the wood
Might stand and rest himself a mite,
Then quickly would be off in flight,
Crossing mountain, field, and lake,
Bidding the drowsy world awake.
Every hour some sleepyhead
Would hear his song and leap from bed[1]
To open his eyes on some delight
Of lovely day or beauteous night.

What would *you* give to see alive
A Wakeupworld at half past five?
Could anything excite you more
Than seeing him at exactly four,

[1]Christopher: That is, all would except that bore,
        That lazy one, that Sleepamitemore,
        Who still would sleep and snore and snore!

His eyes of white, blue, green, and red,
Leaping like carlights from his head?
Or watch each eye from hour to hour,
Beginning at exactly one,
Unfold its beauty like a flower,
Till all those eyes were on the sun?
'Twould take you half a day at least
To get the most of such a feast![1]
But never shall his like appear
Again, and we shall never hear
His song in lovely measures hurled
At sleepyheads throughout the world.

Excitement robbed him of his breath,
Excitement led him to his death.
Flood morning when he could have been
(Being awake) the first one in,
Excitement made him play the dunce
And open all his eyes at once!
He rushed right on through dawn and dark
Pointing late comers to the Ark.
Too great the strain was for his heart;
Slowly he sank; his great knees shook,
While those his song had helped to start
Passed on without a backward look.

The waters fell upon him there,
His twelve bright eyes shining like one;
They covered him, and none knew where
To find him when the storm was done.

[1]Christopher: He'd be the prize of any Zoo,
      If he were here, I think, don't you?

The-Snake-That-Walked-Upon-His-Tail

How envied, how admired a male,
The-Snake-That-Walked-Upon-His-Tail!
The forest all emerged to stare
When he came out to take the air.
With bright eye flashing merrily,
He seemed to say, "Come, gaze on me!
Behold as near as animals can,
A walk resembling that of man!"
And holding high his haughty head,
He would stroll on with graceful tread.
And how his tiny little ear
Would throb these compliments to hear:
"What charm he has!" "What elegance!"
"The ideal partner for a dance!"
"However do you think he learned?"
At this, although he blushed and burned
To tell them how, he never turned,
But, looking neither left nor right,
Would wander on and out of sight.

But why indeed was he so gifted?
By what strange powers was he lifted
A little nearer to the skies?
The reason's plain. Hard exercise!
Hard exercise, indeed! You shake
Your head, and think, "When did a snake,
A creature sleepy and inert,
Content to slumber in the dirt,
Or lie in caverns dank and dark,
Exhibit such a worthy spark?"

But be it found in man or horse,
(Or even snake), a driving force
The fever is we call ambition.
When it attacks, there's no condition
Of man or beast which may withstand
Ambition's hard, compelling hand.

And from his very, very birth,
No common snake was this of ours;
But he was conscious of his worth,
And well aware of all his powers.
He never cared for toads and newts,
For catching flies or digging roots;
No cavern cool could lure him in,
No muddy bank his fancy win.
Wherever man was, there was he!
Eager to watch, eager to see!
He thought it fine that Man could talk,
But finer still that Man could *walk*.
He thought, "If Man can do this, why
With proper training, so can I."

He kept his secret from his nearest
Friend, he never told his dearest,
But in a quiet glade he knew
Where none was apt to come and spy,
The more his perseverance grew,
The nearer did his dream draw nigh;
He practiced patiently and drilled,
And *wished*, and *yearned*, and *longed*, and *willed*.
From crack of dawn to darkest night,

He practiced sitting bolt upright.
At first he fell with a terrible thump,
And bruised his head and raised a bump;
But, "Walk I will!" is what he said,
And lightly rubbed his aching head.

Night after night, day after day,
He would sit up, and sway and sway,
Until one day, oh, think of it!
He stood and never swayed a bit!
He stood as rigid as a pole,
With perfect ease, perfect control!

Though Men should do most wondrous things
In years to come: on iron wings
Fly faster than the fastest bird,
Or talk or sing, and make it heard
Over mountains and over seas,
You must confess that none of these
Could for excitement quite compare
With Snake triumphant standing there
Tip-toe upon his tail! And now
How to begin? He wondered how!

What should he do? Leap? Jump? Or stride?
His heart was hammering inside
Its narrow cell! His throat was dry!
Ambition's fever fired his eye.
Within his grasp he had his dream.
Here was his moment, his, supreme!

Just then he chanced to glance and see
Man passing by, most leisurely;
Step after step Man took with ease,
Eclipsing houses, rocks, and trees.
And suddenly our Snake grew pale,
And whimpered forth a woeful wail;
Till Doomsday though he stood on end,
He would not walk! No need pretend!
One thing he lacked to be complete.
Nothing could walk which hadn't *feet*!

Down, down, he dropped, and sadly crept
Into a bush nearby, and wept.
The tears he shed were sad and salty;
He felt a failure, weak and faulty.
At last, too weary more to weep,
He curled him up and went to sleep.

But some sweet spirit knew his zeal,
Pitied his grief, and sped to heal.
Our Snake's ambitious lower tip
Was caught in some magician's grip,
Till where had been, so sharp and neat,
A tail, were now two tiny feet.
It may have been by wishing so
His earnestness had made them grow!
At any rate, as I repeat,
When he awoke, there were his feet!

He wept again, but now for pleasure!
His joy burst forth in lavish measure.
He popped up straighter than an arrow;
Happiness went bubbling through his marrow!

Then gingerly and cautiously,
And praying Heaven kind to be,
He put his best foot forward! Oh,
It knew exactly where to go!
Without the slightest fuss or bother
Straight behind it came the other.
And from that day until his fall,
He was a wonder to them all.

Pray notice well that last remark,
To wit: "Until his fall," for hark
How too much pride and too much glory
Bring dismal climax to our story.
Our hero, for I still opine
That such he was, though serpentine,
Waxed fat on praise and admiration,
Forgot his former lowly station,
Looked on his mate with mild disdain
As being somewhat soft of brain;
With favor viewed her not at all,
Because, poor thing, she still must *crawl*!
(Which needs no explanation here,
For we believe we've made it clear
That of these two only the Male
Contrived to walk upon his tail.)

The compliments which, left and right,
Were showered on him, spoiled him quite;
No longer friendly and benign,
He strode along with rigid spine,
Nor bent to pass the time of day
Though gently greeted on the way.
Himself he thought the world's last wonder,
All other beasts a foolish blunder,
And even Man he somewhat eyed
A bit obliquely in his pride.

One only thing, or rather two,
He loved with ardor all complete;
Yea, evermore his rapture grew
As he beheld his darling feet!
He bathed them in the coolest brooks,
Wrapped them in leaves against the heat;
He never wearied of the looks
Of those amazing little feet!
And every day, foul day or fair,
Most carefully did count his toes
To be quite certain they were there,
Two sets of five, in double rows.

Flood morning came and Mrs. Snake
Was early up and wide awake.
"Dear husband, rise," she hissed, "the Ark
We must be on and in ere dark."
But he, he only stretched and yawned,
As in his brain an idea dawned
That promised great publicity.

"Suppose, my dear, you go," said he,
"Ahead, and wait on board for me.
Your rate of travel's none too great.
You crawl along; I won't be late."

"True," said his Madam, somewhat tartly,
"I travel as the good Lord made me;
And though I may not travel smartly,
My crawling never has delayed me."
At which in somewhat of a huff,
She straightened out and rippled off.

Quite tardily our Snake arose,
Sat fondly gazing at his toes,
And thought, "The last to catch the boat
I'll be; arrive as one of note.
Perhaps its sailing I'll delay
Almost as much as one whole day;
For certainly they wouldn't dare
To sail away with me not there."

Through all the bustle and commotion
Of others hastening to the ocean,
He gayly spent his time in primping
And polishing his shiny scales,
And laughed to think of others limping
Instead of walking on their tails.

Long, long, he dillied, long, long he dallied,
And dilly-dalliers never yet
Have at the proper moment sallied

To where they were supposed to get.
At length he deemed the proper second
For his departure had appeared;
The fame of being latest beckoned;
For conquest he felt fully geared.

But even as he straightly rose,
And lightly turned upon his toes,
The quiet skies above him darkened.
A panic seized him as he harkened
To thunder rolling long and loud.
Foreboding filled his frame, and dread,
As, glancing up, he saw a cloud
About to spill its contents on his head!
He fled in fright; away he scurried;
From that disturbing spot he hurried.
Yet ever as he onward sped
That cloud still threatened overhead.

At last, at last, he nears the Ark;
'Tis just a little ways away!
Its lights are gleaming in the dark,
It rocks with laughter loud and gay.
"Oh, let me reach it," gasps our hero;
"Though fame and fortune be as zero,
Though none my praises sing aloud,
O Heaven, spare me from that cloud!"

What irony of fate is this?
What bitter fare is his to eat?
Why does our hero writhe and hiss?

Something has tangled up his feet.
A little plant, a sickly bush,
Has grappled with those lovely toes;
Though he may flounder, shove, and push,
No further on our hero goes.
The awful cloud above him tips
And pours its mighty torrents down.
One last look and the captive slips
Away within their depths to drown.
Undone by what he loved the most
He gently renders up the ghost.

Long may his mate stand at the rail,
With anxious eye explore the dark;
The-Snake-That-Walked-Upon-His-Tail
Will never walk upon the Ark.[1]

[1]Christopher: And never, never, in any Zoo
        Excite the wonderment of you!

Dear Friends and Gentle Hearts

We open infant eyes
Of wonder and surprise
Upon a world all strange and new,
Too vast to please our childish view,
Yet love bends down and trust imparts;
We gaze around
And know we've found
Dear friends and gentle hearts;
Good-day, we smile, dear friends and gentle hearts;
Good-day dear friends and gentle hearts.

When on the western rim
Of time the sun grows dim,
And dimly on the closing eye
Fadeth the earth, the sea, the sky,
How blessedly this breath departs
If it pass out
While watch about
Dear friends and gentle hearts;
Good-night, we smile, dear friends and gentle hearts;
Good-night, dear friends, and gentle hearts.

April 1943

Lines for a Hospital

Ye blind, ye deaf, ye mute! Ho, here's healing!
    Here's light to brim
    The eyeball dim;
    Here's sound to cheer
    The muted ear;
    Ways to oppose
    The wayward nose,
    And make sweet notes
    From locked throats
Like chimes cascading come, all pealing:
    Ho, here's healing.

November 1943

A Negro Mother's Lullaby

(After visiting John Brown's grave)

    Hushaby, hushaby, dark one at my knee;
    Slumber you softly, nor pucker, nor frown;
    Though some may be bonded, you shall be free,
    Thanks to a man . . . Osawatamie Brown.
        His sons are high fellows,
        An Archangel is he,
        And they doff their bright haloes
        To none but the Three.

    Hushaby, hushaby, sweet darkness at rest,
    Two there have been who their lives laid down

That you might be beautiful here at my breast:
Our Jesus and . . . Osawatamie Brown.
     His sons are high fellows,
     An Archangel is he,
     And they doff their bright haloes
     To none but the Three.

Hushaby, hushaby, when a man, not a slave,
     With freedom for wings you go through the town,
     Let your love be dew on his evergreen grave;
     Sleep, in the name of Osawatamie Brown.
     Rich counsel he's giving
     Close by the throne,
     Tall he was living
     But now taller grown.
     His sons are high fellows,
     An Archangel is he,
     And they doff their bright haloes
     To none but the Three.

Lake Placid, N.Y.
August 1941

Karenge ya Marenge*

Wherein are words sublime or noble? What
Invests one speech with haloed eminence,
Makes it the sesame for all doors shut,
Yet in its like sees but impertinence?

*Do or die . . . Gandhi

Is it the hue? Is it the cast of eye,
The curve of lip or Asiatic breath,
Which mark a lesser place for Gandhi's cry
Than "Give me liberty or give me death!"

Is Indian speech so quaint, so weak, so rude,
So like its land enslaved, denied, and crude,
That men who claim they fight for liberty
Can hear this battle-shout impassively,
Yet to their arms with high resolve have sprung
At those same words cried in the English tongue?

August 19, 1942

Christus Natus Est

In Bethlehem
On Christmas morn,
The lowly gem
Of love was born.
Hosannah! *Christus natus est.*

Bright in her crown
Of fiery star,
Judea's town
Shone from afar:
Hosannah! *Christus natus est.*

While beasts in stall,
On bended knee,
Did carol all

Most joyously:
Hosannah! *Christus natus est.*

For bird and beast
He did not come,
But for the least
Of mortal scum.
Hosannah! *Christus natus est.*

Who lies in ditch?
Who begs his bread?
Who has no stitch
For back or head?
Hosannah! *Christus natus est.*

Who wakes to weep,
Lies down to mourn?
Who in his sleep
Withdraws from scorn?
Hosannah! *Christus natus est.*

Ye outraged dust,
On field and plain,
To feed the lust
Of madmen slain:
Hosannah! *Christus natus est.*

The manger still
Outshines the throne;
Christ must and will
Come to his own.
Hosannah! *Christus natus est.*

Christmas 1943

La Belle, La Douce, La Grande

France! How shall we call her belle again?
Does loveliness reside
In sunken cheeks, in bellies barren and denied?
What twisted inconsistent pen
Can ever call her belle again?
Or douce? Can gentleness invade
The frozen heart, the mind betrayed,
Or search for refuge in the viper's den?
How shall we call her douce again?
Or grande? Did greatness ever season
The broth of shame, repudiation, treason?
Or shine upon the lips of little lying men?
How shall we call her grande again?

Has history no memory, nor reason?
What land inhabited of men
Has never known that dark hour when
First it felt the sting of treason?
Petain? Laval? Can they outweigh
By an eyelash or a stone
The softest word she had to say,
That sainted soul of France called Joan?

Nay even now, look up, see fall
As on Elisha Elijah's shawl,
Joan's mantle on the gaunt De Gaulle:
New Knight of France, great paladin,
Behold him sally forth to win
Her place anew at freedom's hand,
A place for France: la belle, la douce, la grande.

July 10, 1944

To the Swimmer

Now as I watch you, strong of arm and endurance,
    battling and struggling
With the waves that rush against you, ever with
    invincible strength returning
Into my heart, grown each day more tranquil and
    peaceful, comes a fierce longing
Of mind and soul that will not be appeased until, like
    you,
I breast yon deep and boundless expanse of blue.

With an outward stroke of power intense your mighty
    arm goes forth,
Cleaving its way through waters that rise and roll, ever a
    ceaseless vigil keeping
Over the treasures beneath.

My heart goes out to you of dauntless courage and spirit
    indomitable,
And though my lips would speak, my spirit forbids me to
    ask,
"Is your heart as true as your arm?"

The Modern School, May 1918

I Have a Rendezvous with Life

I.

I have a rendezvous with life,
In days I hope will come,
Ere youth has sped and strength of mind;
Ere voices sweet grow dumb;
I have a rendezvous with life,
When spring's first heralds hum.

II.

It may be I shall greet her soon,
Shall riot at her behest;
It may be I shall seek in vain
The peace of her downy breast;
Yet I would keep this rendezvous,
And count all hardships sweet,
If at the end of the long white way,
There life and I shall meet.

III.

Sure some will cry it better far
To crown their days with sleep,
Than face the wind the road and rain,
To heed the calling deep:
Though wet nor blow nor space I fear,
Yet fear I deeply too,
Lest Death shall greet and claim me ere
I keep Life's rendezvous.

Manuscript, 1920

In Praise of Boys

(Hoping it will evoke an answer from the ladies.)

Thank God for boys!
For the urge in them and the surge in them,
For the god that stifles the dirge in them,
And laughs at the height of the stars;
For their devil-may-care, insolent air,
Hiding the grim, deep places where
Bruises and red wounds are.
The past is proud of its part in them,
Today finds its soul and its heart in them,
And tomorrow stands eagerly by,
Wanting the men she'll find in them,
The brain and the brawn and the mind in them,
Strength of limb and ardor of eye.

Thank God for boys!
For the men they make, and the reins they take
Of enterprise and rule;
Thank God for the wise who philosophize,
And don't forget the fool.
For thinker and dreamer, for plodder and schemer,
For fighter and brawler and ne'er-do-well;
For the ones who roam, who will some day come
Bloody and battered back from hell;
For the worst of them and the best of them,
For the glad and the sad and the rest of them;
For their swaggering gait in the teeth of fate,
For their nonchalant equipoise;
For their pride in life and their scorn for death—
Thank God, thank God for boys!

The New York Times, June 26, 1922

Christ Recrucified

The South is crucifying Christ again
    By all the laws of ancient rote and rule;
    The ribald cries of "Save yourself" and "Fool"
Din in his ears; the thorns grope for his brain,
And where they bite, swift springing rivers stain
    His gaudy, purple robe of ridicule
    With sullen red; and acid wine to cool
His thirst is thrust at him, with lurking pain.

Christ's awful wrong is that he's dark of hue,
    The sin for which no blamelessness atones;
    But lest the sameness of the cross should tire,
    They kill him now with famished tongues of fire,
And while he burns, good men, and women, too,
    Shout, battling for his black and brittle bones.

Kelley's Magazine, October 1922

Dad

His ways are circumspect and bound
    With trite simplicities;
His is the grace of comforts found
    In homely hearthside ease.
His words are sage and fall with care,
    Because he loves me so;
And being his, he knows, I fear,
    The dizzy path I go.

For he was once as young as I,
	As prone to take the trail,
To find delight in the sea's low cry,
	And a lone wind's lonely wail.
It is his eyes that tell me most
	How full his life has been;
There lingers there the faintest ghost
	Of some still sacred sin.

So I must quaff Life's crazy wine,
	And taste the gall and dregs;
And I must spend this wealth of mine
	Of vagrant wistful legs;
And I must follow, follow, follow
	The lure of a silver horn,
That echoes from a leafy hollow,
	Where the dreams of youth are born.
Then when the star has shed its gleam,
	The rose its crimson coat;
When Beauty flees the hidden dream,
	And Pan's pipes blow no note;
When both my shoes are worn too thin,
	My weight of fire to bear;
I'll turn like dad, and like him win
	The peace of a snug arm-chair.

The Crisis, November 1922

A Prayer

Lord, grant me this
Out of Thy power to grant,
That I may ever practice
The creed I cant.
Lord, lead my feet
In paths the just in Thee have trod,
And let my steps be sure, and fleet
To find my God.

Lord, help me speak
The truth, nor fear what wrath recur,
Conscious that grace for those who seek
Thy ways, is sure.
Lord, help me find
And do each day some deed of love.
And by each task my heart to bind
To Thee above.

Lord, let me not
Grind out in vain my span of days,
By friend and foe alike forgot,
Unknown to praise,
But let me live,
Not as a bright king-star to shine,
But humbly, freely, let me give
What gifts are mine.

Lord, leave me not
If tempted I should stray Thy path,·
Nor from Thy love this frail form blot

In righteous wrath,
But mercy have;
Reveal the error of my way,
Then Thou who canst destroy or save
Point me the day.

And help me feel
Thou wilt not slight my feeblest call,
That Thou in joy or woe or weal
Art all in all.

The Southwestern Christian Advocate,
January 4, 1923

A Life of Dreams

My life is woven all of dreams
Like some rich-patterned tapestry,
Whose shift and change and subtle gleams
Are parts of pagan pageantry;
And some are high and fierce and sweet
With wild forbidden loveliness,
And some, the soul's entrenched retreat,
Are calm with strength in holiness.

I call my dreams my dahlia walk
With row on row of colors pied,
With here and there a crownless stalk
Where some ill-tended bloom has died.
Flame-tipped like stars some coruscate
With fire for soul and hungering brain,

And some wear sombre robes, sedate
In agony and splendid pain.

The indices of each day's life
I call them out to suit each mood;
A gay, bright dream to match with strife,
A grave, wise one for solitude.
With some I ride the sun and moon,
Explore infinities of skies;
But some I mount fail all too soon;
Then with his dream the dreamer dies.

I prize them all, swift dreams and glad
Whose grand desire no stint may cure,
The dreams of hope, of lass and lad,
Which only last because they're pure,
But through them all there runs a chord
Whose self is harmony and truth;
Of all the dreams that I've adored,
I love the ageing dream of youth.

The Southwestern Christian Advocate,
February 1, 1923

Road Song

This will I say today,
	Lest no tomorrow come:
Thy words are singing birds
	That strike my faint lyre dumb.

This will I vow thee now,
　　Lest vows should go unsaid:
Thou art unto my heart
　　A song to wake the dead.

This oath I take to break
　　When fails the lover's code:
To fare as thou, and share
　　With thee each winding road.

Thus do I deal my seal,
　　No alien one may break:
Thy mouth to mine, as south
　　The long lone trail we take.

The Crisis, February 1923

Villanelle Serenade

(*"And at dusk on the following day, the prince came
to the foot of the tower and cried:
　'Rapunzel, Rapunzel,
　Let down your golden hair.'"*)

Love to love must make its stair
Out of wind and mad desire;
Love, let down your tangled hair.

Rose and rambling bud may fare
Climbing veins of living wire;
Love to love must make its stair.

Silken webs of light to snare
Soul and body to your hire,
Love, let down your tangled hair.

Lark and swallow pair by pair,
Wing their way while I aspire;
Love to love must make its stair.

Heaven drops no ladder where
Feet of mine sink down in mire;
Love, let down your tangled hair.

Trembling on my lips a prayer,
Let me rise to you through fire:
Love to love must make its stair;
Love, let down your tangled hair.

The Crisis, April 1923

Singing in the Rain

The grass bends low, the pregnant trees
Bend down like men too full in years;
The rain with dull monotonies
Beats time, and gives the willow tears.
That night goes tense as a padded thief
Whose feet in haunted ways are lead,
Or as bereaved who dam their grief
For fear their woe will reach the dead.

With rhymeless drip the sloping eaves
Intone a lay, a subtle mock
Whose cadence weird no whit relieves
The tuneless measure of the clock.
But in some glade faun-tenanted,
A lone bird sings of love and pain.
(Oh heart in sorrow garmented,
There's hope while song can hush the rain.)

Ethereal and clear it soars,
A cherub burst of harmony
That floods the night's gloom-mantled pores
With mellow waves of melody;
Now high, now low, cascades of trills
That climb the stars in a grand finale,
And, loving earth, caress the hills,
And echo long in the windy valley.

On heaven's milky balustrade
Leans wistful, longing Israel;
Whose heart-stringed lyre has never played
Celestial tunes so sweet and well.
And I am somewhere worlds away
In God's rich autumn tinted lanes,
Where, heart at ease from life's dismay,
My soul's high song beats back the rains.

The Southwestern Christian Advocate, May 1923

From Youth to Age

Age, you have failed! With wars and words
    Of mighty sound you sought to win
A world to peace; like wounded birds
    Your plans come home; Age, take them in.

We do not censure you who flung
    Away your strength, your wounds must smart
Who failed to hear in every tongue
    The common language of the heart.

Still, on the wall the finger writes,
    "Your weight holds not the balance down!"
And he who fails, though well he fights,
    Is not fit King! Give youth your crown.

To War and Hate that sever friends
    We pay no further youthful toll,
But, armed with love, we aim to cleanse
    The inner altars of the soul,

Till, purged of littleness of mind,
    We look into our brothers' eyes,
And crying, "Brother," weep to find
    God's self and peace that never dies.

Manuscript, May 4, 1923

The Poet

Poet, poet, what is your task,
Here mid earth's grief and pain?
"To bid them go to distant realms,
Nor enter here again."

Poet, poet, what want you here
Where all is toil and care?
"To sing sweet strength into your limbs
That each his cross may bear."

Poet, poet, what do you ask
As pay for each glad song?
"Full guerdon mine if you but love
My tunes, and love them long."

Poet, poet, what old refrain
Is it that rings so sweet?
"A simple line—Life after Death—
And time has eager feet."

Poet, poet, where will you go
At last, fire crowned and shod?
"Upward at length, a sapphire star,
I'll send forth rays for God."

The Southwestern Christian Advocate,
November 8, 1923

Sweethearts

They talk the silent night away,
    But speak no word by day;
One is a cedar trim and tall,
    His love a willow small.
The one stands proud with head held high,
    The other, coyly shy;
The cedar's limbs are hard and strong;
    The willow's voice is song.

By day when she would love to talk
    Across the garden walk,
The cedar's rude as rude can be,
    Pretending not to see;
And then the willow turns away,
    And sulks throughout the day;
Sometimes she gives a little sigh,
    And once I saw her cry.

At night when our harsh words are said,
    And I am in my bed,
I hear in sweetest harmonies
    The language of those trees.
I find the ivied balcony,
    Where through the gloom I see
Two sweethearts in the yard below,
    Whose speech all lovers know.

The Crisis, December 1923

When I Am Dead

Love, I would have you weep when I am dead,
Would have you show some sign of grief; be sad,
Despair, lament the joys we two once had,
And wail, regretting, love, that all have fled
With me, your all; and grieve that thorns instead
Of flowers tend your way; say nought can make you glad;
Disband your dreams and name each fancy bad,
When I am gone, to whom your soul is wed.
Yea, I would have you weep, for well I know
Spring comes again with warmth to melt the snow;
And lying there your tears shall water me,
Shall drench my form, my face shall warmly wet,
And then when comes the spring, when you forget,
I'll smile to know *some* tears were shed for me.

Opportunity, December 1923

To W. E. B. Du Bois

"The Fledgelings to the Eagle"

Men raised a mountain in your path,
    Steep, perilous with slime,
Then smouldered in their own hot wrath
    To see you climb and climb.

By some black charm they whirled a stream
    Before you for their whim;
You cried, "For faith and the beckoning gleam,
    Limbs, let me plunge and swim!"

"—To fly, we grant such height; no more.
    Be static, that perch won."
"A trial flight, but now I soar,"
    You said, "Up to the sun."

They came to you and said: "This book
    Confines your hire and wage."
Your hand flashed up; you bade them: "Look!"
    And lo! There was no page!

No cultivated plot could bait you,
    No subtly planned disaster;
You were your "Kismet," you your fate, you
    Outmatched them, proved their master.

                    * * * *

This age of mine cries: "Draw no morals,
    For there you quench the fire,—"
Yet what your perch and what your laurels
    Had they no spark to inspire?

Strong eagle, we, the fledgelings, try
    Our wings, though thinly spun,
Because we know you watch, and cry
    Us "Courage!" from the sun.

In the program for a dinner honoring Du Bois,
Café Savarin, New York, April 13, 1924

Night Rain

I wake to the sound of a soft, low patter
   That comes like sudden news,
Or like the slow, uncadenced clatter
   Of well-filled wooden shoes.

I know I have not waked for long,
   That I shall dream again,
That God has sent a slumber song
   Of dew and drowsy rain.

I hear it rush the willows through,
   And strike the garden gate;
Far off a love bird's plaintive coo
   Is answered of its mate.

The night rain works a subtle charm
   Day showers never know;
It makes me burrow deep and warm
   Beneath my sheets of snow.

It brims the pansy's eager cup,
   It dives to the oak's dank roots,
Inquisitive, meanders up,
   And climbs to the newest shoots.

It drips a melancholy tune
   As plunging fierce and deep,
It scurries wild across the moon
   To steep my eyes in sleep.

The Crisis, February 1925

Three Hundred Years Ago

Three hundred years ago there was a land
    And two who moved
With one fair thought: meet hand with hand,
    And to be loved.
Then came a ship and strange, pale men
    Who gave me drink
That made me sleep; I woke—and then—
    The broken link.
I am not sure that you were moved
    At all, or wept;
For you were young and much beloved—
    Perhaps you slept.
But there was blood, and sweat, and hell,
    And tears for me,
Till one whose voice was like a bell
    Said, "Go, be free!"
The chains were off, but other things
    Still held me slave:
A stretch of land where gray and white sand clings
    To a warm white wave.
But more than this, there was your face,
    Beautiful and wise—
Oh, I have sought them every place,
    Your face and eyes.
Three hundred years ago, and yet
    A day ago;
There still the red suns flare and set,
    The dark winds blow.

The Crisis, April 1925

A Sonnet

(*For James Weldon Johnson*)

Thank God I come of those who from the cradle
Are lashed until they totter to the tomb,
To whom Time with a long, ironic ladle
Gruels his worst. Praise God that in the womb
The valiant egg was rounded, warned of this,
Into no pampered progeny of ease,
To wilt and pine, and perish for a bliss
Withheld; think not to see me grovel, please.

An inquisition of the soul and heart
Has shaped my days, and still is casting them;
All-steeled in hurt, of pain a privy part,
Wedded to wounds as light is to the gem,
A scholar capped and gowned in misery,
How thinkest thou, poor world, to harry me?

In a letter to Johnson, May 14, 1931

Song

The blossom quivers on the branch,
The leaves grow restless on the bough,
The sap leaps high from branch to branch,
Flushing the feeblest fragile bough.

The cold-eyed serpent's mind recoils,
(Flame for a space in the calloused heart)
So do your frail hands wind and coil
About the fibers of my heart.

Manuscript, c. 1932

Sonnet

Not knowing what or whom or why I wept,
Yet have the hot and bitter tears prevailed.
Striving the black night through, while others slept,
Not knowing what deep sorrow I assailed,
Uncognisant of what immortal grief
Withheld the haggard body from its rest,
Distress has been my comfort's petty thief,
Despair the shrivelled mistress on my breast.
Aware of only this: that in the core
Of this elusiveness of heart and brain,
Some sorrow not of flesh, nor of this shore,
Beat in the blood a symphony of pain,
Till holding all things hollow, false and cheap,
It was a quaint and quiet joy to weep.

The North Carolina Poetry Review,
November 1933

To Edward Atkinson

Because I voice this mild complaint,
Don't think I'm mad, because I ain't;
I'm just a wee bit roiled and riled
At your indifference, my child.
If you were sick and I were well,
I'd swell the stores of A. G. Bell;
I'd do no disappearing trick,
If I were well, and *you* were sick.
I have no malady outrageous,
Nothing infectious or contagious.

If you should give my hand a shake,
There's nought with which you would outbreak.
If you should come and wish me well,
That would not sound your final knell.
If you should stand beside my bed,
And lay a cool hand on my head,
I think my ills would disappear
As quick as that, yes instanter;
And you would find no rash infection
Resulting from such close connection!
Then there's the phone; I will admit
The fees are rising bit by bit,
But surely, child, you can afford
One little jingle, 'pon my word!

Because I voice this mild complaint,
Don't think I'm mad, because I ain't.*

*But, damn it, I am hurt!

In a letter to Edward Atkinson,
December 3, 1941

Give Them the Second Front

Fear not the Red!
Has he not proven
By the bright blood shed,
By the masses slain
On field and plain,
Who bravely bears the brunt?
Give him the Second Front!

Fear not the Red!
Will honor let us
Distribute words instead?
For a thousand years
Shall we harvest tears
Because he bore the brunt?
Give him the Second Front!

Fail not the Red!
For who has given
Nobler, worthier dead?
Lest our own souls' eyes,
Condemn and despise,
Relieve him of the brunt!
Give him the Second Front!

Fail not the Red!
His battle is our own;
His cause to ours is wed.
Lest Swastikas fly
The Universe Sky,
We, too, must share the brunt!
Open the Second Front!

New Masses, August 11, 1942

Apostrophe to the Land

O land of mine, O land I love,
    A Worm gnaws at your root;
Unless that Worm you scotch, remove,
    Peace will not be the fruit.

Let Hirohito be dethroned,
    With Hitler gibbet-high,
Let Mussolini, bloody, stoned,
    Be spaded deep in lye;

Destroy these three by rope or pyre,
    By poison, rack, or blade,
By every destruction dire
    The Christian mind has made;

Yet while the Worm remains to gorge
    Upon the nation's tree,
There is no armor we may forge
    To fit Peace perfectly.

Rend, rend the Swastika in twain,
    The Rising Sun deform;
But our own flag, shall it remain
    The garment of the Worm?

Is there no hand to lift it free
    Of that miasmic kiss;
The kiss of hate and bigotry,
    The seal of prejudice?

Is there no knight of burning zeal,
	No gifted Galahad,
In accents of redemptive steel
	To cry, "Rejoice! Be glad!"?

Goliath's David long is dust;
	From what heroic sperm
Shall come the deep and valiant thrust
	To slay the loathely Worm?

The little men with slanting eyes,
	They know our pedigree,
They know the length of the Worm that lies
	Under the lynching tree.

The men with strides that ape the geese,
	They know the nation's thorn:
How one man will his brother fleece,
	And hold his hue in scorn.

From Berlin, Rome, and Tokyo,
	The gibing flashes run:
"That land's good picking for the crow,
	Whose people are not one."

Not till the poll tax perishes
	With peons of the South,
And all that hatred cherishes
	With blatant, twisted mouth;

Not till the cheated cropper thrive
    And draw his first free breath
(Though court and custom still contrive
    His legalistic death);

Not till the hedges fall, the moats
    Be mirrors for the stars,
And fair hands drop from darker throats
    Shall we extinguish Mars.

O land of mine, O land I love,
    The Worm gnaws at your root;
Unless that Worm you scotch, remove,
    Peace will not be the fruit.

                    Phylon, Fourth Quarter 1942

Tout Entière

(*From the French of Charles Baudelaire*)

Came Satan to my chamber bare
  Today, with cunning step and slow,
Seeking my reason to ensnare
  In speaking thus: "Fain would I know

Among the gracious attributes
  Whereby she holds you and inspires,
Color of rose or earth-black roots
  In loveliness the universe desires,

Which do you hold most dear?" My soul
    Responded thus to Lucifer:
"Since she is Beauty's parts made whole,
    I find no part I may prefer.

Ravished by all, how shall I know
    What single charm seduces me,
She dazzles hot as sunbeams' glow,
    Like night to calm reduces me.

Too perfect is the harmony
    In which her beauty is confined
For mind to guess or eye to see
    By what accord it is designed.

O mystic metamorphosis,
    Which does my every sense consume!
Her breath most fragrant music is,
    Her voice melodious perfume."

In a letter to Edward Atkinson,
August 12, 1943

A Smiling Africa Speaks

Their gods, ye said, are wood and stone,
    Their bloody altars reek,
Where human hearts lie thickly strown
    In ruddy pile and peak.

For such as they Hell's caverns gape
    And Hell's bright fires burn,

O unredeemed who shall escape,
　　Unless God's grace they learn?

Though somewhat singed in hue they are,
　　God's own they are as we,
And He would have us be the star
　　That guides them to the tree.

For the Lord your God, in whose name ye came,
　　To whom we gave our trust
God of the Cross, of wrath, and flame,
　　Is Jealous, Great, and Just.

Composition notebook, c. 1943

Unfinished Chronicle

I am a man whom deeds affright,
Not one to crave the sun's harsh light;
Mine be the dim protective gloom
Of pen and desk in a little room,
Yet there are some whose meat and drink
Are light and love, and the dizzy brink!
Some strive (as I with pen perspire)
With passion. 'Ware! Beware the fire!

Across the court from where I sit
A play unfolds with verve and wit.
I'm half ashamed to look that way
Who've brought no ticket for the play.

But where the drop is ever up,
Where is the scribbler will not sup,
When summoned steadily to dine
On drama's bright and bubbling wine?

The cast, a slim producer's joy,
The lines will brilliantly employ
The art of any stellar three:
A man, his maid, another he.
Sober the main protagonist
Yet with a tender twist
Bespoken in the awkward pat
He nightly gives the household cat.

His years are large, yet sans that theft
Which leaves the agèd stark, bereft
Of any longing for the flesh.
He is a man, a man's his wish!
Somewhere—was it in dog or doe,
Or frightened child knee-deep in snow?
Some hurt I've seen epitomize
The awful hunger of his eyes.

Hunger for her who wears his ring,
Yet is not his in anything.
And she? She's young; she's fair; she's fire;
The object of two men's desire.
Her gaze is slant, would not be tried
If it were labeled almond-eyed;
Does not deny a Mongol strain
Nor lost completely in the main

Tumultuous tide that makes her an
(Include one part of African)
Unqualified American,
No pallid blossom she, and wan,
But flower cleaving through the rock
Of dark and bright and yellow stock;
In sooth she's young, she's fair, she's fire;
Well worthy of two men's desire.

And he, the villain if you wish,
Third dipper in this toothsome dish?
Evil should wear a proper guise,
A mocking mouth and lecherous eyes;
Have in its gait nought to commend,
Nor any grace to draw a friend.
Nay! He is young and debonair,
And truth, they make a pretty pair.

Her thoughts are all for him tonight,
The heady young cosmopolite,
And just the very shade of brown
To match her olive through the town!
He's schooled in every foppish grace
For bringing blushes to a face
That never thaws save raised to him.
He knows what words in corners dim

Are best invested to declare
The beauty of her eyes and hair.
He's not a thing of stone or wood
Would God the man she married could
Send such a singing through her blood

(Beat of pulse and heart's mad thud)
As this man's soft obsequious lips
Can, brushed across her finger tips!

Composition notebook, c. 1943

Hillburn—the Fair

God have pity
On such a city
Where parent teaches child to hate;
God looks down
On such a town
Where Prejudice the Great
Rules drunkenly
And evilly
What should be Liberty's estate.

The People's Voice (New York),
October 30, 1943

Mad Song

(A provincial Southern air as sung by Senator Rankin and coterie)

Before I'd let a nigger vote,
Or match me place for place,
With my own hand I'd cut my throat
To spite that nigger's face.
I'd raise my hand in Holy Heil

March with the Nazi knee to knee;
Niggers may be Americans,
But Hitler's white like me.

New Masses, May 30, 1944

Modern Mother Goose

Simple Simon,
Wastes his time on
Promises and pledges,
Here a knick and there a knack—make wedges.

But Prejudice a tall tree is
And Lincolnian must be the blow
To bring a tall tree low
To strike its root, and bring it low.

Composition notebook, c. 1944

Modern Mother Goose (As Shaped by Events)

Baa-baa, black soldier,
What are you fighting for?
Freedom for the white man,
And freedom for his dam,
And freedom for the white child,
The snowy, fleecy lamb!

Composition notebook, c. 1944

Elegy

(In Memoriam: Jacques Roumain)

Bring laurel here,
Bring rose
Bring here the tear
That gently flows
For more than earth can bear to lose.
This earth on which he did and said
The things a good man says and does,
Will never think of him as dead,
Nor speak of him as one who *was*.
His spirit lives in light & mist
Nor seeks remoter sphere,
While Time & Memory exist.
Bring laurel here!

Composition notebook, c. August 1944

BIOGRAPHICAL NOTE

The circumstances of Countee Cullen's birth and early up-bringing remain undocumented and obscure. He was probably born Countee Lucas on May 30, 1903, in Louisville, Kentucky. When he was about nine years old, his mother—probably Eliza-beth Thomas Lucas (c. 1884–1940)—sent him to New York to live with his grandmother (or family friend?), Amanda Porter, a day care worker. He entered P.S. 27 in the Bronx under the name of Countee Leroy Porter. After his grandmother died in Decem-ber 1917, he was informally adopted by the Reverend Frederick A. Cullen, pastor of the large and influential Salem Methodist Church in Harlem, and his wife Carolyn Belle Mitchell. He be-came "Countee Cullen" (his Christian name pronounced and sometimes spelled "Countée," as it is on his tombstone), and in later years claimed New York City as his birthplace, revealing the truth about his origins only to intimates. Beginning in 1918, Cullen attended DeWitt Clinton High School, where he ex-celled: he edited *The Clinton News* and the school literary maga-zine *The Magpie*, won oratorical contests, and was elected vice president of his senior class. (He "stuck his finger in every pud-ding," according to his yearbook.) In 1921, he won a citywide poetry contest for "I Have a Rendezvous with Life," which was reprinted in New York newspapers. In 1922, he entered New

York University on a Regents Scholarship. He became friendly with Langston Hughes (then at Columbia) and philosopher Alain Locke (at Howard), and began publishing poetry in *The Crisis* and other national publications. He was increasingly lauded for his poetry, which won many prizes; his first book, *Color*, was published in 1925 to wide acclaim. Graduating Phi Beta Kappa from NYU, he finished his education at Harvard, where he earned an M.A. degree in 1926. In the summer of the same year, he traveled to Europe and the Middle East with his adoptive father, beginning an annual tradition: they crossed the Atlantic together regularly until the outbreak of World War II. After Harvard, Cullen joined the staff of *Opportunity* magazine, serving for two years as assistant editor, and contributing a regular column, "The Dark Tower." He also edited *Caroling Dusk: An Anthology of Verse by Negro Poets* (1927). His second and third books of poetry, *Copper Sun* and *The Ballad of the Brown Girl*, were published in the same year. In 1928, Cullen married Nina Yolande Du Bois, daughter of W.E.B. Du Bois, in a Harlem ceremony attended by thousands. Privately, Cullen's affections were oriented toward men rather than women, and the marriage ended in divorce in 1930, the couple having spent only a few months together. Cullen lived abroad in 1928, 1929, and 1930, mainly in Paris, where he finished *The Black Christ and Other Poems* (1929) on a Guggenheim fellowship. (Also for the Guggenheim, he began collaborating with composer William Grant Still on an opera, *Rashana*, based on an unpublished novel by Grace Bundy Still, but abandoned the project.) On his return to the U.S., he traveled widely, giving lectures and public readings, and finished a novel, *One Way to Heaven* (1932). The novel received favorable but relatively few reviews, and sold poorly. Faced with dwindling earnings from his literary endeavors, he sought a salaried position, and considered offers of professorships from Dillard University and other schools outside of New York. Instead, he began teaching English, French, and creative writing at Frederick Douglass Junior High School, where he continued to work for the rest of his life. Beginning in 1932, he collaborated with novelist Arna Bontemps on a dramatic adaptation of Bontemps's novel *God Sends Sunday* (1931), later to be titled *St. Louis Woman*. He published *The Medea and Some Poems* in 1935; his translation of *The Medea* was later repeatedly adapted for the stage, and its choruses performed in 1943 to music by Virgil Thomson. He also published two books of children's verse, *The Lost Zoo* (1940) and *My Lives and How I Lost Them* (1942). During the summer of 1940, he proposed to his longtime friend Ida Mae Robertson ("If you are willing to overlook and understand my deficiencies, and not to be too disgusted with a husband who can't stand the lightning," he wrote). They wed in October, and after a few years in Harlem moved to suburban Tuckahoe, New York. In 1945, Cullen traveled to Los Angeles, where he worked on revisions to the script of *St. Louis Woman*, attended auditions, and gave readings. He died on January 9, 1946, of kidney failure, after a sudden illness. In March, *St. Louis Woman* opened on Broadway, and ran for 113 performances. In August, *Theater Arts* published *The Third Fourth of July*, a one-act play he had written with Owen Dodson. His selected poems, *On These I Stand*, was published in 1947.

NOTE ON THE TEXTS AND ILLUSTRATIONS

Countee Cullen published five books of poetry during his life-time—*Color* (1925), *Copper Sun* (1927), *The Ballad of the Brown Girl* (1927), *The Black Christ and Other Poems* (1929), and *The Medea and Some Poems* (1935)—along with a book of children's verse, *The Lost Zoo* (1940). Before his death in 1946, he helped to choose the contents for a book of selected poems, published posthumously as *On These I Stand: An Anthology of the Best Poems of Countee Cullen* (1947); he had also written poems that he did not include in any of his books, some published in periodicals, and others left in manuscript.

The present volume includes all of the poems Cullen published in his five books, in the order in which they originally appeared (omitting only Cullen's prose translation of Euripides's *Medea*). From *The Lost Zoo* (1940), it reprints the two poems, "The Wakeupworld" and "The-Snake-That-Walked-Upon-His-Tail," that Cullen later chose to reprint in his volume of selected poems, *On These I Stand*. From *On These I Stand* itself, the present volume contains six poems newly collected in that book. Cullen published all of his books with Harper & Brothers in New York; the texts in this volume have been taken from the first printings of each collection.

The section of "Uncollected Poems" includes, in approximate chronological order of composition, twenty-two poems which Cullen published only in periodicals, and nine poems he left unpublished. Of these unpublished poems, one, "To Edward Atkinson," has appeared subsequently in a scholarly article (Alden Reimonenq, "Countee Cullen's Uranian 'Soul Windows,'" *Critical Essays: Gay and Lesbian Writers of Color*, ed. Emmanuel S. Nelson [Binghamton, New York: Harrington Park Press, 1993], pages 160–61); eight are believed to be published for the first time in the present volume.

The following is a list of the sources from which Cullen's uncollected poems have been taken. *Amistad* denotes items from the Countee Cullen Papers, Amistad Research Center at Tulane University, New Orleans, Louisiana; *Beinecke*, items from the Countee Cullen Collection, Yale Collection of American Literature, Beinecke Rare Book and Manuscript Library, Yale University; *Minnesota*, items from the Countee Cullen correspondence, Givens Collection of African American Literature, Special Collections & Rare Books, Elmer L. Andersen Library, University of Minnesota.

To the Swimmer: *The Modern School* 5 (May 1918): 142. Published under Cullen's earlier name, Countee L[eroy]. Porter.

I Have a Rendezvous with Life: ms. *Beinecke*, from a group of manuscripts Cullen sent to editor Nora Holt during her tenure at the literary magazine *Music and Poetry*, c. 1921. The poem was published in *The Magpie* in January 1921, and in New York newspapers, with some variation.

In Praise of Boys: *The New York Times*, June 26, 1922, p. 12.

Christ Recrucified: *Kelley's Magazine* 1.2 (October 1922): 13. Item from Cullen-Jackman Memorial Collection, Atlanta University Center, Robert W. Woodruff Library, Box 112, Folder 11.

Dad: *The Crisis* 25 (November 1922): 26. First published in *The Magpie* 21 (January 1922): 91.

A Prayer: *The Southwestern Christian Advocate*, January 4, 1923, p. 4.

A Life of Dreams: *The Southwestern Christian Advocate*, February 1, 1923, p. 9.

Road Song: *The Crisis* 24 (February 1923): 160.

Villanelle Serenade: *The Crisis* 25 (April 1923): 277. Published without title in the column "The Looking Glass," as a reprint from *Telling Tales*, a periodical not examined for the present volume. The title is supplied from a draft typescript, *Minnesota*.

Singing in the Rain: *The Southwestern Christian Advocate*, May 1923, p. 8.

From Youth to Age: ms. *Minnesota*, May 4, 1923, inscribed to "Guillaume" [William Fuller Brown Jr.]. Cullen's 1923 "Scrapbook I" (*Amistad*) contains an unidentified but apparently published version titled "Youth to Age."

The Poet: *The Southwestern Christian Advocate*, November 8, 1923, p. 1.

Sweethearts: *The Crisis* 27 (December 1923): 80.

When I Am Dead: *Opportunity* 1 (December 1923): 377.

To W. E. B. Du Bois: menu and program of "Dinner in honor of Dr. W. E. Burghardt Du Bois, Café Savarin, New York, N.Y., April 13, 1924." Beinecke Library, Yale University (James Weldon Johnson Collection).

Night Rain: *The Crisis* 29 (February 1925): 165.

Three Hundred Years Ago: *The Crisis* 29 (April 1925): 279.

A Sonnet (For James Weldon Johnson): ms. *Beinecke*, in a letter to James Weldon Johnson, May 14, 1931.

Song: ms. *Beinecke*, in a letter to Carl Van Vechten, July 1942: "This must have been written about ten years ago. To date it has not appeared in any book or magazine."

Sonnet ("Not knowing what or whom or why I wept"): *The North Carolina Poetry Review* 1.5 (November 1933): 2.

To Edward Atkinson ("Because I voice this mild complaint"): ts. *Beinecke*, in letter to Edward Atkinson, December 3, 1941. Title supplied for the present volume.

Give Them the Second Front: *New Masses*, August 11, 1942, p. 4. Published without title in "Attack Now: Statements to New Masses from Prominent Americans"; the title has been supplied from Cullen's manuscript of the poem (*Amistad*) dated July 30, 1942.

Apostrophe to the Land: *Phylon* (Fourth Quarter 1942): 396–97.

Tout Entière: ts. *Beinecke*, in letter to Edward Atkinson, August 12, 1943.

A Smiling Africa Speaks: ms. composition notebook, *Amistad*, c. 1943.

Unfinished Chronicle: ms. composition notebook, *Amistad*, c. 1943.

Hillburn—the Fair: *The People's Voice* (New York, New York), October 30, 1943. Published without a title in a letter to the editor of *The People's Voice*, and then in an undated mimeographed broadside, with the title and with music by Waldemar Hille (1908–1995). Also published in *PM*, October 28, 1943.

Mad Song: *New Masses*, May 30, 1944, p. 8.

Modern Mother Goose: ms. composition notebook, *Amistad*, c. 1944.

Modern Mother Goose (As Shaped by Events): ms. composition notebook, *Amistad*, c. 1944.

Elegy: ms. composition notebook, *Amistad*. Published in a French translation as "Élégie (In Memoriam: Jacques Roumain)," in *Cahiers d'Haïti* 2 (Novembre 1944): 37, but no English-language publication is known to be extant.

The texts of the original manuscripts and printings chosen for inclusion here are reprinted without change, except for the correction of typographical errors and slips of the pen. Spelling, punctuation, and capitalization may be expressive features, and they are not altered, even when inconsistent or irregular. The following is a list of errors corrected, cited by page and line number: 27.4, that I; 30.9, unremittant; 43.4, face; 77.10, borne,; 93.22, Shelly; 98.6, *Withorne*; 115.12, down; 126.9, venemous; 131.6, eerie; 137.1, Depore,; 150.21, long?"; 177.29, God head; 178.29, pean; 195.9, Euminedes; 211.2, *Louys)*; 219.8, animal's; 240.14, find.; 245.8–9 [no stanza break]; 245.17, [indent] On; 249.26, "Limbs,; 253.10, witheld (and *passim*); 260.16, perfume.

On the following pages, a stanza break occurs at the bottom of the page (not including pages in which the break is evident because of the regular stanzaic structure of the poem): 25, 31, 57, 162, 168, 172, 197, 219, 221, 222, 223.

———

The frontispiece of this volume, a photograph of Cullen taken around 1925, is from the James Weldon Johnson Collection, Yale Collection of American Literature, Beinecke Rare Book Room and Manuscript Library, Yale University.

On pages xxxvi, 92, 120–121, and 124, this volume reproduces some of the illustrations, by Charles Cullen (c. 1889–?), in Countee Cullen's first four books of poetry. The two men were "not related" (as the poet explained in a letter of October 1927 to Kathleen Tankersley Young); indeed, the illustrator was "not even colored." According to Gwendolyn Bennett, writing in *Opportunity* in September 1927, Charles Cullen's father, interested in things associated with the name "Cullen," had sent his son a copy of the first edition of *Color*. The illustrator introduced himself to the poet, who persuaded his publisher to commission Charles to illustrate *Copper Sun*. The success of that collaboration led to a newly illustrated second edition of *Color* in 1928 and to illustrated editions of *The Ballad of the Brown Girl* and *The Black Christ and Other Poems*. For further information about the collaboration between the two, see Caroline Goeser, *Picturing the New Negro: Harlem Renaissance Print Culture and Modern Black Identity* (Lawrence: University Press of Kansas, 2007).

NOTES

In the notes below, the reference numbers refer to page and line of this volume (the line count includes titles and headings, but not spaces). Biblical references are keyed to the King James Version. For further information and references to other studies, see: Gerald Early, ed., *My Soul's High Song: The Collected Writings of Countee Cullen, Voice of the Harlem Renaissance* (New York: Doubleday, 1991); Blanche E. Ferguson, *Countee Cullen and the Negro Renaissance* (New York: Dodd, Mead, 1966); Thomas E. Jenkins, "An American 'Classic': Hillman and Cullen's *Mimes of the Courtesans*," *Arethusa* 38 (2005): 387–414; Michael L. Lomax, "Countee Cullen: From the Dark Tower" (Ph.D. diss., Emory University, 1984); Charles Molesworth, *And Bid Him Sing: A Biography of Countée Cullen* (Chicago: University of Chicago Press, 2012); Margaret Perry, *A Bio-Bibliography of Countée P. Cullen, 1903–1946* (Westport, Connecticut: Greenwood Publishing, 1971); Alden Reimonenq, "Countee Cullen's Uranian 'Soul Windows,'" *Critical Essays: Gay and Lesbian Writers of Color*, ed. Emmanuel S. Nelson (Binghamton, New York: Harrington Park Press, 1993); Alan R. Shucard, *Countee Cullen* (Boston: Twayne Publishers, 1984); and James W. Tuttleton, "Countee Cullen at 'The Heights,'" *The Harlem Renaissance: Revaluations*, ed. Amritjit Singh, William S. Shiver, and Stanley Brodwin (New York: Garland Publishing, 1989).

1.1   *Color*]   In the original printings of *Color*, Cullen included a dedication: "To my Mother and Father / This First Book."

6.18   *Yolande*]   Nina Yolande Du Bois (1900–1960), daughter of W.E.B. Du Bois, graduated from Fisk University with a fine arts degree in 1924. She married Cullen in April 1928 in a massive ceremony: more than a thousand people crowded the church, and another thousand gathered outside. The marriage ended in divorce by 1930. Du Bois later remarried and worked in Baltimore as a high school teacher.

7.19   *Roberta*]   Roberta Bosley (also spelled Bosely), later Roberta Hubert (b. 1906?), was a cousin of Cullen's by adoption. She grew up in Philadelphia, but by the early 1920s was working as an assistant librarian at the 135th Street Branch of the New York Public Library (now the Schomburg Center for Research in Black Culture); she later headed the library's children's services program. As founder of the James Weldon Johnson Literary Guild, she served as host and promoter of many Harlem literary events, and was active in raising funds for the NAACP. After Cullen's death, she collaborated with Carl Van Vechten and Harold Jackman in assembling his papers for posterity.

9.18   *Atlantic City Waiter*]   Cullen himself worked as a waiter in Atlantic City's Traymore Hotel, as he explained to his friend Harold Jackman in July 1923: "It is by no means a position, just a job, but it gives me time to study some of the vermin of the race, and since three-fourths of every race is vermin, I am in with the masses. Donald [Duff] would love this atmosphere, but my bourgeois soul receives it as one takes an emetic— with disgust. The place has inspired two poems. For that the vermin be praised!"

11.2   *Donald Duff*]   Born in London to American parents, Duff (1903–1941) was an actor and playwright affiliated with the *Liberator*. Cullen refers affectionately to Duff in letters to Alain Locke and others around 1923–24, and later defended his play *Stigma* (1927, with Dorothy Manley Duff) against negative reviews (the *Times*' critic called it a "sophomoric play of miscegenation"). Duff lived in Paris during the 1930s, returning to New York when war broke out in Europe.

12.5   *Simon the Cyrenian*]   Simon, Jesus' cross-bearer (see Luke 23:26), has traditionally been represented as a black man, and was the subject of Ridgely Torrence's 1917 all-black play *Simon the Cyrenian*.

13.2   *Eric Walrond*]   Born in British Guiana (now Guyana), Walrond (1898–1966) moved to New York in 1918 and attended City College and Columbia University. He worked as associate editor of the Garveyite magazine *Negro World* from 1923 to 1925, and as business manager for *Opportunity* from 1925 to 1927; in 1926, he published *Tropic Death*, a collection of short stories. In 1930, both having received Guggenheim Fellowships, Cullen and Walrond briefly shared a studio in Paris.

16.10   *René Maran's "Batouala"*]   *Batouala* (1921), by the Martiniquan René Maran (1887–1960), was the first novel by a writer of African descent to win the Prix Goncourt.

21.2   *Llewellyn Ransom*]   Ransom (1900?–1972?) was a student of Alain Locke's at Howard University with whom Cullen may have been romantically involved in 1925; to Locke, Cullen wrote, "L. is a godsend. And I don't forget your part in directing the gift my way." Ransom had a brief career on the stage, performing in the Harlem musical revues *Rang Tang* (1927) and *Hot Rhythm* (1930), after which he worked as a correspondent and photographer for the *Pittsburgh Courier*, the *Philadelphia Tribune*, the *Chicago Defender*, and other papers.

22.6–7   Or hast Thou . . . in a bush for me?]   See the story of Abraham and Isaac in Genesis 22:1–14.

28.2   *Harold Jackman*]   Jackman (1901–1961) attended DeWitt Clinton High School with Cullen, and became a lifelong friend; to Alain Locke, in 1924, Cullen wrote, "I feel toward him as David toward Jonathan." The best man at both of Cullen's weddings, Jackman worked as a model and a journalist to supplement his income as a teacher, and was prominent in Harlem social life. He founded the Harlem Experimental Theatre Company in 1929, and helped to edit the magazines *Challenge* (1934–37) and *Phylon* (1944–61).

33.2   *For a Poet*]   Cullen added a dedication to this poem in the 1928 second edition of *Color*, "To John Gaston Edgar." Edgar (1904–1996), a native of West Virginia, graduated from Columbia University and later worked for the Community Service Society of New York, an anti-poverty organization. He published a short story in the *West Virginia Review* in 1924, but his poetry is not known to have appeared in print.

39.17   Not writ in water]   Keats (1795–1821) wanted his tombstone (in the Protestant Cemetery, Rome) to bear only the inscription "Here lies one whose name was writ in water."

40.1   *Hazel Hall*]   Hall (1886–1924), who lost the use of her legs as a child, was the author of poetry collections *Curtains* (1921), *Walkers* (1923), and the posthumous *Cry of Time* (1928).

40.6   *Paul Laurence Dunbar*]   Dunbar (1872–1906) was the leading African American poet in the generation prior to Cullen's and the author of *Lyrics of Lowly Life* (1896). Cullen may allude to his poem, "We Wear the Mask," from that collection.

42.3   *Ruth Marie*]   Ruth Marie Thomas, later Ruth Marie Thomas Hargrave (1903–1967), was a close friend and correspondent of Cullen's for over twenty years. As a teenager, in 1920, she interviewed actor Charles Gilpin for the NAACP children's magazine *The Brownies' Book*; she went on to receive her doctorate in education from New York University in 1946, and was a longtime faculty member at Wilberforce College. In 1945, she edited the anthology *Spices: Selected Readings by Negro Authors for the Young Adolescent*.

44.2   *Guillaume*] Cullen's pen name for William Fuller Brown Jr. (1904–1983), a high school friend and longtime correspondent with whom he shared poems in manuscript. Brown later attended Cornell and Columbia and worked as a research physicist and professor of electrical engineering.

48.6   *Ottie Graham*] Ottie Beatrice Graham (b. 1900?), educated at Howard and Columbia, wrote the one-act plays *Holiday* (1923) and *The King's Carpenter* (1926), and contributed stories to *The Crisis* and *Opportunity*. She performed as Acté in the Howard Players' 1921–22 production of Ridgely Torrence's *Simon the Cyrenian* (1917), for which she helped to arrange the choreography.

49.1   *Judas Iscariot*]   As published in *Color*, this poem differs substantially from an earlier version that appeared in the *Southwestern Christian Advocate* in March 1923.

52.18   *Alain Locke*]   Locke (1886–1954) was chairman of the philosophy department at Howard University and a leading editor and anthologist of African American literature. The two began an extensive and intimate correspondence during Cullen's first year at New York University. They later met in Washington, and Locke joined Cullen and his father during vacations in Europe.

55.1   *Col. Charles Young*]   Charles Young (1864–1922) was the highest-ranking African American in the U.S. military when he died of a tropical fever while on active duty in Nigeria. He was eulogized by W.E.B. Du Bois and Franklin D. Roosevelt.

57.2   *Carl Van Vechten*]   Van Vechten (1880–1964), a writer and photographer, was a leading white patron of Harlem Renaissance writers. In 1925, he helped Cullen to publish a group of his poems in *Vanity Fair*. Cullen "turned white with rage" (in Van Vechten's words) on hearing the title of his 1926 novel *Nigger Heaven*, and their friendship cooled, but the two remained in touch until Cullen's death.

58.24   *Willard Johnson*]   Walter Willard ("Spud" or "Gipsy") Johnson (1897–1968), of Taos, New Mexico, edited the influential little magazine *Laughing Horse*.

59.10   *Walter White*]   Walter Francis White (1893–1955) joined the staff of the NAACP in 1918, and served as its executive secretary from

1931 until his death. He published a best-selling novel, *The Fire in the Flint* (1924), studies of lynching (*Rope and Faggot*, 1929) and military segregation (*A Rising Wind*, 1945), and a memoir, *A Man Called White* (1948). White was an early supporter of Cullen and his work, and helped him to make contacts in the publishing world.

61.1   *Copper Sun*]   When he first published *Copper Sun*, Cullen included a dedication: "To the Not Impossible Her."

61.4   *Charles S. Johnson*]   Johnson (1893–1956), a sociologist trained at the University of Chicago, became national research director for the National Urban League in New York in 1922. In 1923, he founded *Opportunity: Journal of Negro Life*, for which Cullen later served as assistant editor (1926–28), and to which he contributed a regular column, "The Dark Tower." Johnson went on to join the faculty of Fisk University and to write many books, including *Shadow of the Plantation* (1934), *Growing Up in the Black Belt* (1941), and *Patterns of Negro Segregation* (1943).

66.5   *Colored Blues Singer*]   This poem was originally published in the magazine *Folio* in 1923, under the title "Blues Singer." It included a penultimate stanza which Cullen later omitted: "Sure if your man could hear you now / No other wanton's charms / Could conjure up a magic how / To keep him from your arms."

67.1   Jeritza]   Maria Jeritza (1887–1982), a celebrated Moravian soprano. She performed at the Metropolitan Opera from 1921 to 1932.

67.6   *Leland*]   Leland B. Pettit (b. 1901), an organist who moved to New York from Milwaukee, is said to be represented in several Harlem Renaissance *romans à clef*: as Mark Thornton in Blair Niles's *Strange Brother* (1931), Samuel Carter in Wallace Thurman's *Infants of the Spring* (1932), and Leslie in Bruce Nugent's *Gentleman Jigger* (written c. 1933, published 2008). Thurman, in a February 1926 letter to Langston Hughes, describes him as "quite a friend of Countee's too I believe or *was*"; in September 1929, Harold Jackman reported to Cullen: "there is a rumor in Harlem that Pettit committed suicide—I spoke to your father about this and he said it wasn't true. But the niggers have it that Pettit committed suicide over some boy."

70.3   *Fiona*]   Fiona Braithwaite, later Fiona Carter (1906–1990), was the daughter of anthologist and literature professor William Stanley Braithwaite. In April 1926, Cullen wrote to Harold Jackman: "my passion is not concentrated, but divided between Miss Sydonia Byrd and Miss Fiona Braithwaite . . . Rumor has already engaged me to both the young ladies who share my unstable affections; so that for the first time in my life I feel what it means to be a sheik—even if only on a small scale."

71.3–12   Abelard . . . Lancelot]   Famous lovers from history, legend, and opera.

81.16–17   Elaine . . . Astolat]   In Arthurian legend, Elaine died of unrequited love for Lancelot; her story inspired Tennyson's "The Lady of Shalott" (1833/42).

82.15   *Ruth Marie*]   See note 42.3.

84.2   *Robert S. Hillyer*]   Hillyer (1895–1961) was one of Cullen's professors of poetry at Harvard; he later won the Pulitzer Prize in Poetry for his *Collected Verse of Robert Hillyer* (1933).

93.17   *Cor Cordium*]   Heart of hearts.

95.8   *John Trounstine*]   John Jacob Trounstine (b. 1903?) was a New York literary agent who at various points represented Arna Bontemps, Erskine Caldwell, Langston Hughes, Dorothy West, and Richard Wright; he also published translations of German literature.

96.2   *Amy Lowell*]   Lowell (1874–1925) was a leading imagist poet and a posthumous recipient of the Pulitzer Prize in Poetry for *What's O'Clock*. Like Cullen, she was a devotee of John Keats, publishing a two-volume biography, *John Keats*, in 1925.

98.6   *Emerson Whithorne*]   Whithorne (1884–1958), a composer, set a number of Cullen's poems to music, including "Saturday's Child," "A Song of Praise," and "To One Who Said Me Nay" in *Saturday's Child* (1926, for mezzo-soprano, tenor, and chamber orchestra), and "The Love Tree," "Lament," and "Hunger" in *The Grim Troubadour* (1927, for medium voice and string quartet).

100.14   *Edward Perry*]   Edward G. Perry (c. 1908–1955) was appearing in the 1927 London run of Dorothy and DuBose Heyward's *Porgy: A Play* when he first met Cullen. In the following year, he served as a groomsman at Cullen's wedding, reporting on the event for the *Pittsburgh Courier*. He later worked as a reporter, music critic, casting director, and party planner for socialite A'Lelia Walker and others (he was "Harlem's male Elsa Maxwell," according to *Jet*). During World War II, he led the USO touring unit of *Porgy and Bess*.

102.2   *Sydonia*]   Sydonia Byrd (b. 1905?), a native of Indianapolis and a student at the New England Conservatory of Music. See note 70.3.

104.4   Cressid]   In postclassical accounts of the Trojan War, Cressida is a beautiful Trojan woman who forsakes her lover Troilus for a Greek soldier; her name became synonymous with inconstancy.

104.18   *John Haynes Holmes*]   When it first appeared in *The Crisis* in March 1927, this poem was prefaced with a note: "Read at the Testimonial Dinner to John Haynes Holmes in recognition of his twenty years as

Minister of the Community Church of New York City." Holmes (1879–1964) was a pacifist and a proponent of nonviolent social protest.

106.15   Your humble epitaph]   See note 39.17.

113.1   *The Ballad of the Brown Girl*]   In the original paintings of *The Ballad of the Brown Girl*, Cullen included a dedication "To Witter Bynner"; Bynner (1881–1968), an American poet, author, and scholar, remembered especially for his translations of Chinese poetry, lived most of his life in Santa Fe. Cullen won the 1925 Witter Bynner Undergraduate Prize for the poem while he was a student at New York University. Bynner was one of the prize judges, along with Carl Sandburg and Alice Corbin, and he later became friendly with and corresponded with Cullen.

125.3   *the Three for Whom the Book*]   Cullen included a dedication in the original edition of *The Black Christ*: "A Book / for Three Friends / EDWARD / ROBERTA / HAROLD." The friends were Edward Perry (see note 100.14), Roberta Bosley (see note 7.19), and Harold Jackman (see note 28.2).

130.18   *Lynn Riggs*]   Rollie Lynn Riggs (1899–1954), part-Cherokee playwright, poet, and screenwriter, traveled to Europe in 1929 on a Guggenheim fellowship, just as Cullen did. His plays included *Big Lake* (1926), *Roadside* (1930), and *Green Grow the Lilacs* (1931), the last of which was subsequently adapted in the musical *Oklahoma!* (1943). He also worked as a screenwriter, sharing credit for *Garden of Allah* (1936), *The Plainsman* (1936), and other films, and published a book of poetry, *The Iron Dish* (1930).

140.12   *Ultima Verba*]   Last word.

161.1–2   *Black Majesty . . . Vandercook's chronicle*]   See *Black Majesty: The Life of Christophe, King of Haiti* (1928), by John W. Vandercook (1902–1963).

161.4   Christophe and Dessalines and L'Ouverture]   Henri Christophe (1767–1820), Jean-Jacques Dessalines (1758–1806), and François Dominique Toussaint L'Ouverture (1743–1803), leaders of Haiti.

161.15   "Lo, I am dark . . . Sheba sings.]   See the Song of Solomon 1:5 (for Sheba's words), and 1 Kings 10 (for Sheba's visit to the kingdom of Solomon).

164.6   Dothan's hill]   See 2 Kings 6:17, where the prophet Elisha invokes God's aid against the Syrian army.

165.2–3   the sun . . . stopped in Gibeon]   See Joshua 10:12–14.

195.3–4   *a Visit . . . Irish poets*]   Cullen attended a gathering hosted by Irish American writer Padraic Colum (1881–1972) in Paris in February 1930.

205.8   *for D. W.*]   Probably Dorothy West (1907–1998), a close friend and correspondent. West had published short stories and would go on to write two novels, *The Living Is Easy* (1948) and *The Wedding* (1995); she founded and edited the magazine *Challenge*, and worked as a journalist.

211.1–2   *Bilitis Sings . . . Louÿs*]   See *Les Chansons de Bilitis* (1894), by Pierre Louÿs.

211.19–20   *Death to the Poor . . . Baudelaire*]   See "La Mort des Pauvres" in Baudelaire's *Les Fleurs du Mal* (1857–61).

212.12–13   *The Cat . . . Baudelaire*]   See "Le Chat" in *Les Fleurs du Mal*.

213.1–2   *Cats . . . Baudelaire*]   See "Les Chats" in *Les Fleurs du Mal*.

213.17   Scottsboro]   On March 25, 1931, nine black youths, aged thirteen to twenty, were accused of raping two young white women on a freight train in northern Alabama. They were tried in Scottsboro, Alabama, beginning on April 6, 1931, and on April 9 eight of the defendants were sentenced to death; the cases were appealed to the Supreme Court, and became a cause célèbre.

217.28   Christopher]   Christopher Cat, who is credited, along with Cullen, as coauthor of *The Lost Zoo*, from which this poem is taken. In "A Word about Christopher," which introduces the collection, Cullen writes: "Cat is not only Christopher's last name, but Christopher *is* a cat, a real cat, colored white, and orangey. Christopher belongs to me, or maybe I belong to Christopher."

229.3   *Dear Friends and Gentle Hearts*]   This poem was set to music by William Lawrence and published as sheet music by Chappell & Co. in 1943. The title phrase is borrowed from Stephen Foster (1826–1864); it was found written on a scrap of paper in Foster's wallet after his death.

230.19   Osawatamie]   Also spelled Osawatomie, a town in Kansas Territory settled by abolitionists who hoped to gain Kansas's entry into the Union as a free state. On August 30, 1856, John Brown (1800–1859) helped to defend the town against pro-slavery forces.

236.1   *I Have a Rendezvous with Life*]   Cullen's poem was written in response to "I Have a Rendezvous with Death" (1916), a widely reprinted poem of World War I, by Alan Seeger (1888–1916).

243.15–18   *"And at dusk . . . golden hair."*]   See "Rapunzel," in *The Red Fairy Book* (1890), edited by Andrew Lang (1844–1912).

253.2   *James Weldon Johnson*]   Johnson (1871–1938)—a diplomat, civil rights activist, and author of *The Autobiography of an Ex–Colored Man* (1912) and *Along This Way* (1933)—was an advocate of Cullen's work, and Cullen had favorably reviewed Johnson's books.

254.18   *To Edward Atkinson*]   Atkinson (1917?–1977?) occupied a primary place in Cullen's affections during his later years. The two corresponded extensively from 1937 until Cullen's death, after which Atkinson donated Cullen's letters to the Beinecke Library. Carl Van Vechten photographed Atkinson extensively during the 1940s: as Saint Martin de Porres, as Young Pushkin, at the Stage Door Canteen, and in his military uniform.

254.24   swell the stores of A. G. Bell]   Use the telephone.

259.14   *Tout Entière*]   From Baudelaire's collection *Les Fleurs du Mal* (1857–61). The French title means "wholly," "completely," "in its entirety."

262.5   a slim producer's joy]   In Cullen's manuscript "an impresario's joy" has been added above this phrase.

264.5   *Hillburn—the Fair*]   In October 1943, white students from the village of Hillburn, in Rockland County, New York, boycotted their newly desegregated school. Cullen's poem was originally published at the end of a letter to the editor of the *People's Voice* (New York), on October 30, 1943. The letter introduced the poem as follows: "Coming home the other night from Stage Door Canteen where democracy is being given a chance to prove itself with Negro and white service men fraternizing as brothers in arms should, I thought what a step backward Hillburn has taken. I think of them in this way."

264.17   *Mad Song*]   This poem was written for "New World A-Coming: An Original Pageant of Hope," performed at the June 26, 1944, Negro Freedom Rally at Madison Square Garden, and attended by some 25,000 people. The pageant was arranged by Owen Dodson (1914–1983), a dramatist and poet who had staged Cullen's translation of *The Medea* in 1940 and collaborated with him on *The Third Fourth of July*, a one-act verse play published in *Theatre Arts* in August 1946.

264.18   *Senator Rankin*]   John E. Rankin (1882–1953), member of the House of Representatives from Mississippi who was noted for his anti-Semitic and segregationist views.

266.2   *Jacques Roumain*]   Roumain (1907–1944) was a noted Haitian writer and politician. He helped to found the Haitian Communist Party in 1934; in 1947, his novel *Gouverneurs de la rosée* (1944) was published in English as *Masters of the Dew*, in a translation by Langston Hughes and Mercer Cook.

INDEX OF TITLES
AND FIRST LINES

AMERICAN POETS PROJECT